THE MAN FROM SPANISH CREEK

by

Logan Stuart

Dales Large Print Books
Long Preston, North Yorkshire,
BD23 4ND, England.

British Library Cataloguing in Publication Data.

Stuart, Logan
  The man from Spanish Creek.

  A catalogue record of this book is
  available from the British Library

  ISBN 1-84262-115-7 pbk

First published in Great Britain in 1957 by
Rich & Cowan Limited

Cover illustration © Faba by arrangement with
Norma Editorial S.A.

The moral right of the author has been asserted

Published in Large Print 2001 by arrangement with
Roxy Bellamy, care of Watson, Little Ltd.

Dales Large Print is an imprint of Library Magna Books Ltd.

Printed and bound in Great Britain by
T.J. (International) Ltd., Cornwall, PL28 8RW

CONTENTS

CHAPTER 1

THE PLAN IS BORN

Frank Hervey tooled the buckboard along Main, veering over to a vacant space at the rack outside the Mercantile.

He was a young, slimly built lad, barely out of his teens, good-looking except for the dark eyes which were set a little too closely together, and the stubborn mouth that suggested weakness rather than strength.

The pleasurable anticipation he had felt driving along the trail from Spanish Creek now seemed to evaporate suddenly. Yet, when Dave had told him to take the buckboard into town for a few meagre but essential supplies, he had felt a quick lift of spirits. For one thing, a trip to Wildcat always meant a break in the hatefully monotonous work of the homestead and, apart from that, there was always a chance of seeing Pearl Gallina.

Frank climbed down from the seat, tied reins to the hitchrack and stood undecided on the edge of the boardwalk. Passing folk nodded casually at Ma Hervey's youngest boy and a wave of resentment ran through

Frank as he called to mind the kind of welcome the town's citizens afforded Dave when he was along.

There was something about Dave that commanded a ready respect and Frank knew this without experiencing any prideful thrill. He sensed that just as Nature had denied to him his brother's stature and breadth of shoulders, so also was he lacking in the slow, easy-going and sympathetic attitude which, combined with an inherent strength of purpose and shrewd insight, caused folk to seek Dave's opinion on matters generally. Yes, even though the Herveys were little better than nesters with their fifty-sixty head of scrub cattle, both Ma and Dave seemed to be accorded a respect out of proportion to their station.

Something of young Hervey's bitterness and resentment glittered in his eyes and showed in the sneering scowl which etched itself upon the lean, beardless face. Irritated, he jingled the coins in his pants' pocket, knowing that by the time a few debts had been settled and fresh stores paid for, there would be scarcely the price of a drink left. He shook his head in a gesture of angry frustration. Dave was pretty tight-fisted with the money they made. Not that there had ever been much *dinero* for as long as Frank could remember. And when Pa had been alive, it had been much the same story. Work from sun-up to sun-down and be dam' thankful you had a supper to eat!

With Pa gone, things had improved a little. Jo Hervey had never been much more than a shiftless dreamer and with one less mouth for Ma to feed, the sky brightened a little; not much, but some.

Frank moved slowly now towards the open door of the Mercantile, in no hurry to complete his chores, mind busy as it was. About the only smart thing Jo Hervey had ever done, Frank thought, was to file on the three-twenty acre section on Spanish Creek and have the title legally recorded at Stella, the county town. That way, no one could shift them. Not even the powerful, pushing Walt Dillon, the man who owned Hatchet which sprawled across half of Crooked River Valley; the man who had taken a shine to Ma and rode over every so often to growl out another proposal to the still good-looking Clovis Hervey. Well, Ma was okay, Frank grudgingly conceded, but why in tarnation she didn't up and marry Walt and so make things easier for Dave and himself, was something he couldn't figure.

Dave and he had been running the Hervey homestead right from the time Pa had upped and died on account of him being bitten by a Gila monster and the doc not coming quick enough. If Ma only had the sense to marry Dillon, their financial troubles would be as good as over. But like Dave, Ma was bull-headed when it came to things like that. Maybe she figured he and Dave needed her to boss things. But they didn't. They needed nothing that money couldn't buy, Frank thought bitterly.

He waited his turn to be served by Charlie Schwarz, feeling his face and neck redden when the Mercantile owner asked if that was all.

He emerged from the store, hating every minute of these chores he had to do. Why in hell couldn't Dave had driven in and done this? Maybe with his smiling face and drawling voice he'd have fixed up some further credit with old Schwarz!

Turning down-street towards the livery stables, Frank glimpsed the rotund figure of Sheriff Herb Lack at his desk beyond the open office door. Frank's lips thinned down at sight of Wildcat's fat, balding lawman. He felt nothing but contempt for Herb Lack. The man couldn't catch a robber even if he *witnessed* the crime. Hervey reflected as he turned in through the wide doors of Sam Platt's Feed Barn and Livery.

It was the same story here. Winter grain to pay for and just one new sack to be humped back to the tied buckboard.

The coins in Frank's pocket were dwindling and there were still a few more supplies to purchase. Potatoes, until the Hervey's own first crop were big enough to dig; flour, sugar, a few items of canned goods.

By the time the list had been dealt with and the provisions stowed in back of the buckboard, there remained a paltry four dollars and a quarter. His lips twisted as he recalled Dave's parting remark.

'Anything left over, Frank, is yours. You've earned it. Buy yourself something you fancy in town.' That was what Dave had said. Hell! how far did the fool figure forty dollars went with credit to square and fresh purchases to make!

Even if he *wanted* to spend the rest of the morning drinking, there wasn't enough *dinero* for more than a couple of whiskies!

He leaned against a clapboard wall under the roofed-in boardwalk, pushed back the battered hat and ran fingers through his thick, matted hair. Maybe, if he hoped to see Pearl and make a good impression, he should spend the money at the barber shop and get Max Cassen to chalk up the drinks!

He watched the street, glance darting to the Lucky Strike's batwing doors. A couple of punchers clattered along Main and pulled their mounts to a halt outside the saloon. With a stirring of envy, Frank saw that each wore a filled shell-belt and a holstered six-gun.

He slouched back against the wall, thumbs hooked in his belt. Once or twice his right

11

hand strayed to the region of his side-pocket as though he were easing the weight of a Colt's gun.

Slowly the feelings of frustrated anger and bitterness built up within him to an almost intolerable degree. It was as though a great weight lay upon his chest, pressing down on him, even reaching up to constrict his throat.

He saw the fresh-faced Gilroy Blessiter, son of Wildcat's banker, cross the street and stand outside the Lucky Strike. In a few moments, Pearl Gallina emerged, looking radiantly lovely, sweeping the street with her veiled glance.

Frank half stepped away from the wall, only to haul up abruptly as though he had walked into the side of a wagon.

The smiling Gil Blessiter had removed his hat to Pearl, had offered her his arm and, half coquettishly, half arrogantly, the singer had accepted.

In a mood of impotent rage young Hervey's gaze remained pinned to the couple as they walked along the boardwalk, greeted effusively by men, but coldly by Wildcat's sunbonneted wives and daughters.

For a long time Frank Hervey stood there, still as a rock except for the spasmodic clenching of his leathery hands. It had merely been visual proof of what he had suspected for weeks, but the thought brought no relief, no consolation. A man might kid himself that he was steeled to meet a certain situation, but there was always the wishful hope that the fear would not materialize. When it did, the reactions of anger and shock seemed no less intense because he had anticipated the *dénouement* and had schooled himself, as he had thought.

Gil Blessiter! If Hervey hated any man in Wildcat, it was this jumped-up, dude son of Wey Blessiter. Even at school, and that was not so many years back, Gil had had everything that money could buy. Worse than that, he had always contrived to beat Frank in most things; had licked him at lessons and more than once had licked him with his fists. The social gulf which had stretched between Gil Blessiter and the other children, particularly the ragged-trousered Hervey kid, still lay, but wider and deeper than ever before. And, though Pearl Gallina had talked to Frank as an equal, sometimes more, with a hint of suggestion in her bold eyes and throaty voice, she was more than ready to jump through Gil's hoop, because of the man's clothes, his money and position!

The two Hatchet punchers stepped out through the swing doors and almost with unseeing eyes, Frank watched as they wiped bearded faces with the backs of sun-burned and rope-scarred hands. The holstered guns joggled as they walked bow-leggedly to their racked mounts; the long-rowelled spurs jingled as they dragged over the scuffed boards.

There was something romantic and picturesque about the way these men held themselves, stepping into leather and pulling the low-crowned stetsons down over their eyes against the sun's glare. There was just a hint of danger and toughness there as well. Everyone knew that on Walter Dillon's pay roll was more than one man who had used a gun on another human; and the whole bunch, including Munro Gucht, the ramrod, were rough-and-tumble men.

If Frank had suffered the pressure of bitter discontent on him before and had seethed with jealous anger at sight of Pearl and Gil Blessiter, he now began to experience a sudden mood of grim resolve. Almost to his surprise, an unprecedented determination took hold of him. He was not quite sure yet, what it was all about. This new emotion would need examination. Thoughts, vague and ephemeral at first as the drifting valley mists, entered his mind, softly and gently insinuating themselves into his consciousness.

'You needn't be a down-at-heel, two-bit nester,' they seemed to say. 'Why should you work for Dave and Ma for next to nothing, and to hell with having to stand by while Blessiter walks out with Pearl under your very nose!'

But what to do? Frank asked himself. What chance has a Hervey got of making money and doing the things he wants, especially the younger son? Why, I can't even afford to buy a new shirt or pants. I've got to wear Dave's cast-offs and I'm still stuck with Pa's old hat, the one he was using when he got himself killed!

Frank looked down at his sod-buster's boots, so unlike the scuffed, soft-leather Justins worn by the Hatchet riders. There were tears in his eyes, his mouth trembled and his hands shook. Pity flooded over him. A pity, not for Ma or Dave, but for himself. He choked back the lump in his throat and lifted his blurred gaze and, whether by intent or sheer chance he never really knew, but he found himself gazing at the imposing façade of Wildcat's second brick building, Wey Blessiter's bank! He saw it for the first time as a symbol representing the sharp division between his world and the world of folk like the banker's family. And, inexperienced though he was with women, Frank knew with an intuitive certainty that if Blessiter's bank were to crash, Pearl would drop Wey's son like a hot flapjack.

The thought ran on into the deeper recesses of Hervey's consciousness. He licked lips with a tongue suddenly become dry. He felt trickles of sweat running down his temples and from underneath his arms as he swung his gaze from left to right, absorbing the disposition of the nearby buildings in relationship to the bank itself.

When the idea had fully blossomed in Frank's brain, he felt too staggered and shocked for a few moments to examine it further. His pulses were pounding and his heart-beats seemed to be ringing out with the violence of a steam-hammer.

With a strong effort he composed his face into its normal expression, fearful that the thoughts which had rocked his brain might reveal themselves to passers-by. He began walking towards the lower quarter of the town where itinerants, loafers and bar-flies contrived to exist in almost untenantable tar-paper shacks.

Here, in this comparatively deserted section, he could squat down on his boot-heels and think things out more carefully.

Now that he had given himself time to recover from the mental bombshell of his own creation, he could view the idea a little more calmly and objectively.

To rob Wey Blessiter's bank! That was the sudden thought which had come to him with such unexpectedness and violence!

Supposing, he found himself considering, it *could* be done! Just supposing that he, Frank Hervey, together with someone he could really trust, were to ride up, cool and casual one day an hour or so after noon, the bank's quiet time. His companion would stay with the horses – not Hervey mounts which were not only branded and well known but useless for a fast getaway – while he, Frank, would step through the bank's doors and throw down on old Simon Churt, the teller. It might be as well to figure out a day when Wey Blessiter was away some place. That would leave only Churt to deal with and any chance customers.

Frank reached out for a sliver of wood at his feet, unsheathed his knife and commenced to whittle, as his thoughts raced on.

Such a scheme would need financing before it could be put into operation, and to whom could he turn? Who was there with the ready *dinero* to whom he dare suggest such a plan? Hervey could find no immediate answer to this and pushed the problem temporarily to one side.

All kinds of hitherto undreamed of details would have to be worked out and Frank now felt excitement gripping him as he went over each point as it occurred to him.

The problem of good horses seemed almost as insurmountable as that of finding a partner willing to engage in the hold-up and equip them both.

Although he did not possess a hand gun, Frank was a good shot with a deer rifle and had, more than once, tested and fired Dave's Colts which his brother kept stowed away in oil rags.

He toyed with the idea of stealing one from Dick Maurey's gun-shop but almost immediately rejected such a dangerous plan. If something went wrong, and he were caught, it would ruin his chances for the big thing, the raid which would perhaps net him several hundred dollars and at the same time sink the first few nails into Gil Blessiter's coffin!

Any suggestion that he was not still the dutiful son going about his chores, would have to be kept carefully from Ma and Dave, and that wouldn't be too easy. He would also have to offer Dave a sure-fire, genuine excuse for being away from the homestead at the time of the robbery and also when it came to looking for a likely partner.

Somehow or another, Frank would not only have to get an expensive horse and gun, but would also have to furnish himself with clothes which were not recognizable in Wildcat like the ones he habitually wore. Range-rig, perhaps, with spurred half-boots, checkered shirt and a waddy's wide-brimmed stetson pulled well down to a concealing mask. Even some kind of facial disguise might be necessary he reflected, if he did not want to pull the mask up until the moment of entering the bank.

But what about a clean getaway? Once the robbery had been staged and pulled off, the alarm would be given and even Sheriff Herb Lack was liable to move fast in a crisis.

Frank saw the surrounding country in his mind's eye as he stared at the wood he was busily whittling. Mentally, he traced a line from the side-street adjoining the bank, right out to the more undulating country west, where bush-fringed arroyos and low ridges would give fair protection from a following posse.

The line ran on to the boulder and cañon country only three-four miles away, where Lobo Cañon rose upwards from talus slopes of shale and rock.

Frank's lips split into a grin of satisfaction as he thought about Lobo Cañon. All the folks around claimed it was a box cañon with no outlet. But Hervey knew differently, and, as far as he was aware, was the only one who *did* know of the narrow slit-opening at the far end.

This had been a piece of knowledge stumbled upon accidentally during his schooldays. A secret discovered and, for some reason, jealously guarded and never surrendered to anyone, not even Ma or Dave!

Here at least was one problem solved, or partially solved. The country west of Wildcat was ideal, broken and wild, and once the shale of Lobo Cañon had been reached, no one short of an Injun or Mex would be able to follow their sign further. Even if they did, they were to likely to stumble upon the weed-choked exit two miles from the cañon entrance. Frank himself had only discovered it by the merest chance; a schoolboy's overwhelming curiosity stronger even than fear had compelled him to follow a baby wildcat which, as he figured later, must have wandered from its hide-out during its mother's absence.

He found the lair, well hidden and high up on a rock shelf and luckily for young Hervey, the female did not return until after the boy was long gone.

If Hervey had not been running the baby cat to its home, likely he would not have spotted the all but hidden outlet. As it was, he even urged the pony along the narrow slit to a point where the sparsely wooded brush country opened out ahead.

Several times after that, at intervals through the following years, Hervey had ridden out to Lobo Cañon when the chance had afforded. And he had come to look upon the place as his own retreat. The mountain lion family had long since gone and in fact Hervey had never considered the possible danger from wild animals.

Looking back now to those earlier days, he could even remember something of the terrain beyond the cañon, over which he had ridden more than once. If he were to

ride out there again, he could make a conclusive check on whether Lobo Cañon
could provide a really feasible escape route.
He thought it could.

The obstacles which had yet to be overcome, even before any detailed planning
could begin, might well have caused a
stronger-minded man to discard the whole
project. Oddly enough, the more Hervey
thought about his difficulties, the more ob-
stinately determined he became to eliminate
them and shape his plan accordingly.

Perhaps on the way home, he would think
of some alibi that would satisfy Dave and
Ma with regard to his necessary absences
from the section. Well, today was Saturday
and he was free to go for a ride this
afternoon. Dave allowed him that much
freedom. But even this was not the biggest
problem. That lay in the question of a
partner, horses and guns. Frank knew that
the idea he had bitten off was far too big to
chew on alone. A raid on Wildcat's bank
could be no solo job whatever.

He rose from his hunkered down position
and threw the sliver of half-carved wood on
to a pile of trash. His belly told him that
already it was near to noon and Frank
decided to spend his few dollars at the
Chink restaurant and claim 'expenses' from
Dave. From now on, he would need every
red cent he could lay his hands on!

CHAPTER 2

HOMESTEAD ON SPANISH CREEK

Dave Hervey unhitched the draft horse from the plough shafts and led the animal towards the big barn standing some fifty or so yards from the house.

After he had grained and rubbed down the mare, he moved with an easy swinging gait to the wooden bench on which stood a fresh bowl of water, towel and lye soap.

Dave was a tall man, with wide sloping shoulders and a well-muscled body rendered strong and tough from years of hard, physical work. From the open doorway of the house, Clovis Hervey, or 'Ma' as she was most generally called, watched her eldest son wash up and tidy himself in readiness for the noon meal.

The old and faded linsey-woolsey dress could not entirely hide the young-girl beauty of form which was still hers.

The golden hair of earlier days had become more whitish looking, bleached by the many summer suns. Yet it still retained more than a suggestion of its former silken sheen. Her face, though lined, was well formed, the features pleasingly regular except for a rather wide mouth which, paradoxically, seemed more to harmonize with her looks than contrast with them.

'Seems like Frank is eating in town,' she said, putting her gaze in the direction beyond Spanish Creek.

Dave towelled himself vigorously and nodded before replacing the patched shirt on his back.

'Frank's going to feel mighty mean with me,' he grinned. 'Told him to keep the money left over but I clean forgot the feed bill we owed Sam Platt. Won't be more'n three-four dollars remaining for Frank to play with. Have to make it up to him,' Dave added, stepping up to the doorway.

Ma wiped clean hands on her spotless apron and brushed a lock of hair back from her face; involuntary gestures, as she glimpsed the rider a couple of miles beyond the creek. Dave's glance followed the direction of his mother's.

'Walt Dillon,' he said, and spat.

'Real class folks don't spit,' Ma reproved gently, 'even when they see the King of Crooked River ridin' by.'

'Trouble is,' Dave drawled, 'he's not riding by. He's fixin' to taste some of your fresh-baked pie and between mouthfuls ask you for the twentieth time to marry him.'

A faint colour crept into Ma's wind-tanned cheeks, then receded.

'I've sure told him often enough to save his breath. I wouldn't ever–'

'Why not?' Dave demanded, shaking dry tobacco on to paper and deftly rolling and lighting the quirly. 'About time you started in on thinking of yourself instead of me and Frank. We took over when Pa died and have managed pretty well, though you've done more than a woman's share–'

'Walt doesn't want a wife. He wants–' Ma broke off and bit her lip. Then the ready smile came to the rescue. She was always forgetting that her sons were now grown men, old enough to understand such things. Especially Dave. As for Frank, she supposed she would never really cease to think of him as her baby.

'Howdy, Clovis!' Walt Dillon's voice boomed out as he put the big horse to the creek. Walt showed his dislike of the sobriquet 'Ma', by the consistent use of her proper name.

Ma raised her hand in greeting as Dillon rode across the yard.

'Better light down, now you're here, seein' it's nigh on dinner-time,' she said tartly, turning back into the house.

Dillon's broad face creased into a grin. 'Why, so it must be. I hadn't figured it was that late!'

Dave's smile was entirely without humour.

'What they call a coincidence, eh, Walt?'

Dillon climbed down heavily and tied reins to the hitch-rack.

'Guess you don't like me much, Dave, do you? But you will,' he averred, confidently, 'you will. Guess you got a streak of your ma – your mother's stubbornness.'

'Don't ever go further than that,' Hervey admonished quietly, 'or else I might have to hurt you pretty bad.'

Dillon's eyes were hard and cold as his gaze fastened on to Dave's face. He was, maybe, twenty-odd pounds heavier than the elder Hervey boy, but whereas Walt carried a deal of fat, Dave was all muscle and hard as rock. Young enough, too, the Hatchet owner thought, to move twice as fast on his feet.

For once, Dillon had no ready answer to what was virtually a challenge. He followed Dave inside, trying to shed his annoyance by watching Clovis busy at the stove.

There was no doubt about the quality of Ma's cooking. Tender beef and vegetables, home-baked bread, hot, crusty apple pie and cream all vanished with amazing rapidity.

'Beef was sure good an' tender, Clovis,' Dillon grinned. 'Hope it wasn't a Hatchet cow your boys pulled down.'

'If that's meant to be–'

'Aw, hell, Clovis! I was only jokin'. Don't

take on so. It sure spoils your beautiful face when you scowl like that!'

Ma could see through Dillon just about as clearly as she could through the glazed windows after they'd been washed. Yet, because of his obviousness and in some ways, childlike transparency, she could rarely fail to be amused by the big man. Particularly so when he tried to be placating in his heavy way.

At times like these, when Dillon shared a meal with them or sometimes just a cup of coffee, Ma tried to forget the ugly rumours concerning the cattle baron of Crooked River. And, most generally, because of her sweet nature, she succeeded.

It was only sometimes at nights, in her own small bedroom, that she let her mind dwell on the prospect of marriage with the powerful rancher and then, gossip and rumours that she had heard, would come flooding into her mind, causing her to shiver and, for the moment, hate Walt Dillon with all the strength of which she was capable.

Quite a few times recently, as Walt Dillon's pressure on her had increased, Ma had remembered the young and beautiful Mex girl, Rosita Morales, who had been hired by Hatchet ostensibly as a kitchen help. No one, apparently, had seen the girl alive again and weeks later, clean-picked bones were found in a gully. That, in itself, would have proved little. But the sharp-eyed deputy, Will Fiedler, spotted an Aztec charm close by, which was known to have been one of Rosita's most cherished possessions. There had been no evidence as to how the girl had died, nor who had killed her, if indeed she had been murdered. Sheriff Herb Lack could do no more than shrug his fat shoulders and send in his inconclusive report to Stella, after the coroner had declared an open verdict–

But Ma's thoughts were not running along such dark channels now. Like most women, and particularly those who acquired a more mature charm in middle age, she blossomed in company, even Dillon's, and felt a simple, child-like thrill at the compliments, in spite of seeing through the rancher's motives.

Dave's animosity seemed to have lessened considerably. Over coffee, he discussed cattle with the Hatchet owner, while Ma cleared away the things and paused now and then in her work to make some succinct remark.

'Of course, Clovis,' Walt said presently, 'I'd allus give you a good price for this two-bit section if you was ever minded to sell–'

'What would you be wantin' with Spanish Creek, Walt, with most of the Crooked River Basin for Hatchet stuff?' Ma asked, pouring herself a cup of coffee.

Dillon shrugged. 'I don't *need* it. But I'm not above wantin' to own the only strip of land I can't have. No man would be,' he grinned, 'and I figure the *dinero* would be mighty useful for Dave and Frank to start a *real* spread–'

'We could only do that if you paid about ten times what the section's worth,' Dave drawled. 'Don't tell me any man would do *that*!'

The Hatchet owner flushed. Dave had a nasty habit of getting under his skin. The Herveys sure had a downright, mean, cussed streak in them.

Always, when Walt wanted anything, he had only to reach out a large hand and grab. Money talked and so did power. Things could be fixed. And if that didn't work, most any of the boys, including Munro Gucht, would do a little shooting or fire-raising for a bonus. Pleased to....

The rattle of wheels sounded softly over to the further edge of the creek and Dillon was glad of the interruption.

'It's Frank,' Dave said from the door. 'Guess maybe he'll want another dinner, Ma!'

Frank waved a hand as he tooled the buckboard across the yard and quickly deposited groceries and stores on a bench, leaving the sack of grain aboard.

Dave felt a faint surprise as his younger brother climbed back and drove the rig over to the barn. It was unlike Frank to bother unhitching and tending the shaft horse until he had satisfied his own immediate requirements. Even then, on many occasions, he put off such chores until finally Dave saw to them himself.

But now the boy was even rubbing down the grey, in the barn doorway, feeding it a little alfalfa.

It was both puzzling and pleasing that Frank should return from town with a fresh heart for the kind of chore which he normally despised.

Maybe I've been pushing him too hard lately, Dave thought. *The kid needs more breaks from the work here, even if it's only an extra trip into Wildcat once a week.*

There was a bubbling effervescent feeling inside Frank. It had been with him all the time on the drive back from town and had not subsided with his arrival home.

He felt as he imagined a man might feel after drinking a good champagne, yet, far from being over-boisterous or reckless in his attitude, he seemed imbued with a caution and wariness almost foreign to his nature.

Instead of saying the first thing that came into his mind, he examined each thought carefully before opening his mouth. He was pleased that Dillon was here, for the rancher's presence would provide a kind of screen behind which he could shelter from any undue attention on the part of Ma or Dave.

Besides, Frank rather liked the big cattle man. Walt was scared of no man, knew what he wanted and went out after it. He was the kind of hombre a fellow might do well to pattern himself on. *Maybe it won't be so long now,* Frank thought, as he greeted the others, *before I am tasting a little of the sweetness which Walt has fed on for so long!*

'Nice to see yuh, Frank,' Dillon boomed. 'Better tuck into that pile of food your mother's dished out. I can recommend it!'

Frank grinned. 'You cain't tell us much about Ma's cooking,' he said, seating himself at the table. 'In any case, I'm starved enough to eat a hoss!' He threw a sly glance at Dave and added. 'A man cain't get much of a meal on three dollars!'

'I had that coming to me,' Dave smiled, producing twelve silver pieces and laying them alongside his brother's plate. 'Reckon you've earned that, Frank, and we won't say anything more about the cost of a meal in town.'

Frank flushed with surprised pleasure. He dropped his gaze, fearing as he had done in town, that others might read into his expression that which he had to keep so very, very secret.

But both Dave and Ma saw only a kid's appreciation shining in his face; the natural

30

elation a child exhibits when suitably rewarded for some chore or another.

The senior Herveys were making their first big mistake in continuing to regard Frank as a kid...

Dillon heaved himself to his feet and laid his warm gaze on Clovis. She was annoyed with herself that whilst a part of her resented Walt's intimate glances, another side of her nature warmed to such attentions. She tried hard to keep the picture of Jo in front of her, feeling suddenly wretched that she should even have to try.

'Don't forget what I said about this place,' Walt told her, picking up his hat. 'It wouldn't hurt me to pay you, say seven dollars an acre as against the dollar an' a quarter Jo paid Uncle Sam. Like I said, Dave an' Frank here could start in on some quality breeding with, lemme see – well over two thousand dollars behind 'em –'

Ma's mouth was a little tight as she nodded. 'We'll let you know when we figure on quittin', Walt.'

Dillon let it lay, giving Dave a nod and directing a wide smile at Frank as though only the two of them knew what was what.

The Herveys watched in silence through the open doorway as the rancher climbed aboard and presently rode out of their sight in the direction of Hatchet headquarters.

Frank was the first to break the silence, as

he pushed aside his empty plate and twisted round in the chair. 'You ain't turning down an offer for *that* kind of *dinero,* are you, Ma? Why, I guess you and Dave would be crazy–'

'We don't aim to sell out for *that* kind of *dinero,* or any other kind,' Dave murmured, his eyes on Ma's face. 'We–'

'Listen, boys,' Ma interrupted, sinking on to a hardwood chair. 'You especially, Frank. You don't remember much of your pa, and what you do recollect ain't clear, I guess.

'But *I* remember him from way back, right to the time I first saw him an' knew deep down inside of me that Jo Hervey was the only man I'd ever want to marry.

'Oh, sure,' Ma hurried on, catching a hint of the sneer in Frank's expression. 'You only remember Jo as he was later on. A dreamer, a man who could set down and plan things better'n he could up and do 'em. But don't hold that against him. It was just – well, just the way he was made, I guess. It isn't given to every man to ride roughshod over his neighbours and build up vast herds at other folks' expense.

'I never have spoke to you much about your pa, what he was like when he was a carpenter in Independence and came courtin' the preacher's daughter.' A soft light crept into Ma's eyes and a mistiness was on her dark lashes like dew-drops glistening on a spider's web.

'He brought me out here,' she went on softly, 'because he believed in the land, not only for farming, but cattle as well, like – like Walt Dillon, only the two of them was almighty different kinds of men.

'Jo called Spanish Creek our "promised land". I guess that's why he had sense enough to take up the Government's offer of a dollar and a quarter for every acre. He didn't ever want to leave here, once we was settled, even though he'd 'a' made a sight more money following his trade at every new town that sprung up.

'Well,' Ma sighed. 'Money sure is a lot, but it ain't everything, and don't you boys ever forgit that. I haven't been able to give you much beyond a little schoolin', and some hard lessons in doin' the right thing. There ain't never been much money. I don't haveta tell you that, though we have had a few more things since you boys has run things. But,' she paused, her glance directed through the window at some far-off and non-existent point in the distance, 'I hope I been able to give you *somethin'*, some kind of appreciation for the things that's right. And, your pa had this land in his bones. He sunk his roots into this soil and now he's buried out there beyond the barn, lyin' at peace in the place he wanted to be in, and surrounded by the things and the folk he loved!'

Ma's gaze came back from the far distance with dragging reluctance.

'I didn't aim to make a speech,' she said, and now there was the touch of a smile on her lips and in her grey eyes. 'But don't let any of us get this thing wrong. We ain't figurin' on sellin' out to Walt Dillon, no, nor any other sech man who wasn't good enough to latch your pa's shoestrings!'

'You don't haveta hurt yourself, Ma,' Dave muttered, 'drawin' us a picture. We – Frank and me – understand maybe better'n you figure. We know how hard–'

'I ain't been hurtin' myself, Dave,' Ma said, with shining eyes. 'Does folks a power of good to sometimes remember sech things. God's been good to me, first with Jo an' then with you two.' She shook her head, smiling. 'No, Dave, I ain't a bit unhappy, I got so much to be thankful for.'

To Dave, Ma's revelation was a kind of sacred thing. Like removing your hat in church and like when you were bad hurt or kicked down, you asked His help just the same as He was a pardner standing right alongside you.

To Frank, Ma's words and feelings had little power to penetrate his new-found armour. The armour with which, from now on, he would protect himself against anything that might threaten the successful execution of his plan. Frank's imagination had become so fired by his idea, that he was well-nigh incapable of allowing other considerations, external events, to impinge upon his actively working brain.

'If it's all the same to you, Dave,' he smiled, 'I'd sure like to take a ride and work some of the stiffness outa my arms an' legs. That alfalfa patch I been workin'–'

'Sure,' Dave nodded, coming back to earth with a bump. 'Ma an' me'll do anything that's necessary. You take my hoss, Frank, and ride to Caprock or some place. Buy yourself a shirt and hat if you want.'

It felt fine to have a good saddler under you, instead of the eighteen-year-old shaft horse. Money in your pockets, too! Not much, but more than Dave had dished out in many a long month. Would it be best to buy a new hat and shirt, or was this the opportunity needed to get a gun?

If I did that, Frank mused, *what could I tell Ma and Dave?*

He pushed the problem from him for the moment and gave himself up to the exhilaration of the ride, putting Dave's roan first to a canter, then to a gallop, finally reining it to a steady lope.

The early afternoon sun tinted the snow-capped peaks of the Magpies with a golden-orange light and though men like Frank Hervey were fundamentally unappreciative of such natural beauty, the grandiose sight

35

nevertheless caused an upsurge of spirits in him which made this Western frontier suddenly seem like a land of vast opportunity. Not the kind Pa had dreamed about, but the kind which Walt Dillon had seen, and taken advantage of years back.

But inevitably, Frank's thoughts travelled the complete cycle, until, once again he found himself grappling with the biggest obstacles to his plan. Yet, despite his preoccupation, the boy rode with an eye and an ear tuned to direction. He had no intention of wasting precious spare time joyriding. Thus, he put the roan now to a series of lesser-known trails and cut-offs which brought him to the grassy undulating range west of Wildcat which in turn gave way to the boulder rock of the cañon country three miles away.

Keeping clear of the stage road, Frank followed the direction and route which he had previously lined out in his mind when first considering the idea this morning.

Every now and again, he would turn in the saddle and give his back-trail the benefit of a careful scrutiny, judging how hidden he might be from a posse, say a mile or two away.

He rode on, becoming more and more satisfied with this aspect of the plan, yet aware of the fact that he was concentrating on the getaway before he had begun to plan details of the hold-up itself.

He was perhaps a mile away from the shale stretches footing the cañons, travelling a narrow road on one side of which lay a steep, rock-filled ravine. A sharp incline ahead gave him no more than a fifty-yard view of the road.

He had heard no sound to indicate the presence of other travellers on this less frequented road some way from the main trail. So it was, Frank Hervey reined in sharply atop the rise and gazed down on the scene only sixty or so paces away.

A wagon, a right smart-looking wagon, stood hipshot as it were, on account of the nearside front wheel was missing. A span of Morgans were hitched to the trees, and, judging by the foam on chests and fore-legs, they must have run themselves silly.

At first Frank had assumed the figure bending down over the axle-tree to be that of a small man. Surprise rippled through him now as he noted the fringed buckskin skirt and the long black hair, some of which had become unpinned and lay in disordered array on the girl's bandana-covered shoulders.

At that moment one of the Morgans nickered and Frank's roan answered. The girl swung her gaze round, seeing Frank and fixing him with a hard, unwinking stare, at the same time slowly rubbing the axle grease from her hands on to a rag.

CHAPTER 3

EMMA

'Ef'n yuh ain't too tired, mister, mebbe yuh could climb down off'n thet crowbait an' help me fix this con-blasted wheel!'

Frank returned her stare striving to mask his surprise at the unexpected encounter. In those few seconds of pause, he found himself trying to place this rather wild-looking creature. What was a young woman doing, travelling this country presumably alone? How did such a ill-kempt looking person come to be in the possession of a fine canvas-topped wagon drawn by a team of Morgans?

He saw the spark of anger flash in her dark, beady eyes and quickly swung down, ground-tieing Dave's roan before approaching the damaged vehicle for a closer inspection.

The wheel wouldn't take much fixing. It was just a question of casting around for a fair-sized boulder and a length of timber with which to lever up the axle preparatory to sliding the wheel on. The team was restive, but Hervey thought they had thrown off most of their scare.

He walked round the rear of the wagon to the other side, and checked that the brake was full on. He hitched the trailing reins to the lever and started rolling a large boulder from the trail's edge, manoeuvring it to a position immediately underneath the front axle-tree.

He straightened up and regarded the silent girl coldly. She wasn't being over helpful.

'You got some kind of lever in the wagon?'

She nodded and strode to the tail-gate with almost mannish strides, returning in a few seconds with a stout iron bar some six feet in length.

Frank took it, insinuating the spoon-shaped end underneath the boulder's base. 'Catch hold that wheel an' be ready to run it on when the axle comes up,' he grunted.

The whole operation took little more than a couple of minutes and Hervey found himself grudgingly admiring the deft way in which the girl had shoved the wheel home at the right moment.

He pushed the pin through and cleaned the grease and dirt from his hands, taking his first full and close look at the girl.

She was not above seventeen or eighteen years, he surmised, with a hard, angular face and black eyes about as expressive as a rock lizard's. The sunburned hands were broad and were obviously used to work.

She wore a black, dust-covered stetson, shirt and brush jacket and a fringed doe-skin skirt. The Justins on her feet, though thorn-scarred and unpolished, had been costly to buy.

Suddenly and surprisingly, she produced a Bull Durham sack from the jacket and proffered it to Frank.

He shook his head and grinned. 'Don't use it, miss.'

She gave an almost imperceptible nod, rolled a quirly and placed it between her thin lips. She withdrew a match from the pocket of her brush jacket and fired the paper cylinder.

Frank found it difficult not to stare. Except for an occasion or two when Pearl Gallina had puffed a customer's quirly in the Lucky Strike, this was the first time the boy had ever seen a female use tobacco. He didn't even know that they were capable of such things.

'Reckon yuh bin wonderin' what happened?' she said, exhaling a mouthful of smoke. Frank leaned against the wagon's side, his mind full of unspoken questions. But he schooled himself against the impulse to quiz her, merely nodding.

'Somethin', a rattler, I guess, scared them hosses. Pup was driving with a jug of liquor at his feet.' She paused, turned her head in the direction of the ravine's rim. 'He's down there, someplace. Got throwed clear outa the seat when the wheel broke loose. Ain't nuthin' we kin do,' she added quickly, perhaps sensing that her words had shocked the boy.

'Pup was my step-paw. Ain't known any kinsfolk. I usta cook an' darn fer him–'

'What was he, a whisky drummer?'

She dropped the quirly and toed out the ember. 'Yuh might say that.'

Frank waited, feeling that there was more to come.

She studied him, an intuitive shrewdness helping her to determine and assess the boy's character. She jerked her head indicating for Frank to follow her, and as she wheeled, Hervey saw the Colt's gun tucked into the waist-band of her divided skirt.

Wonderingly he joined her at the rear of the wagon and gazed in astonished silence at what lay stowed away in the wagon-bed.

She had leaned over and tugged at some burlap. Underneath, was a long, open chest containing several gleaming carbines. It was likely, from the size of the chest, that there had been many more rifles stashed there originally.

Beside the weapons' chest, Frank's quick eye took in several smaller ammunition boxes wedged in between crocks of liquor, kitchen utensils, a dutch oven, blankets, and a score of smaller miscellaneous household articles.

41

She was eyeing him intently now and stood poised like a cat making ready to spring. Her right hand was close to the Colt's butt at her waist.

And suddenly, Frank saw the whole picture in clear and detailed perspective! Here, surely, like a bolt from the sky, had come the answer to his problem! What matter that his partner was a young girl? She had shown herself tough and self reliant in her very actions and words. Carbines for the using! And perhaps somewhere in the wagon, even a spare Colt's gun!

Frank stepped back and let out a slow, deep breath. This whole situation was one which he could never have dreamed up in a thousand years. It fitted so exactly, that, for a short space, he could think of nothing to say.

'Whisky an' guns,' the girl said in her low, harsh-sounding voice. 'Mebbe fer white settlers, mebbe fer Injuns was they to pay in gold or greenbacks! But was yuh figgerin' to ride into Caprock an' hunt out a Federal man?'

She had backed away a few paces. The expression on her face was feral. Narrowed eyes glittering, lips drawn back from sharp-pointed teeth, she slowly pulled the six-gun from her waist-band.

Frank felt fear slide over him, crawling along his skin and causing beads of cold sweat to stand out on his face. He knew he had never been so near death in his whole life; that if the girl believed for one moment he was likely to call in a U.S. Marshal, she would think nothing of killing him…

He licked dry lips, forcing a smile which he prayed she would not misinterpret.

'I was figurin'',' Hervey said slowly, in a voice which sounded strained and alien to his own ears, 'that you an' me might well team up. You don't haveta believe this,' he went on more quickly, 'but I've got a scheme laid out that's likely goin' to bring in several thousand dollars – just for ten minutes' work! What I need right now,' he croaked, plunging desperately, 'is a partner with plenty spunk. Someone like you, mebbe, who can use a gun and fork a hoss an' think quick in an emergency.'

He waited, with baited breath, watched the wildness fade from her eyes, to be supplanted by a glitter of bright interest. Slowly, the girl's face lost its honed down look. Her claw-like right hand relaxed as she eased the gun back into place.

But, despite the interest in her sloe-black eyes, disbelief and scorn were etched in the curl of her lip and the thin flare of her nostrils.

'How many suckers yuh tried *that* one on, mister?'

'Ain't had the chance,' Frank replied with

forceful truth, 'seein' as I only started figgerin' the thing out early this morning.'

The shine of a deep scepticism still lay on the girl's face, but Hervey felt a lessening of hostility in her general attitude.

'Why don't yuh pick up this easy *dinero* on your lonesome, mister, 'stead of fixin' to share it, and what kind o' work's so durned well paid yuh kin earn thousands in ten minutes?'

It was a long speech for the girl and when she had finished, she rolled and lit another quirly, gazing out across the range as though her interest in the boy and his crazy idea had all at once subsided.

Frank said quietly, 'Bustin' into a bank needs more'n one to pull it off smoothly. A fella got to have his back watched an' know the hosses are in the right place when he comes out at the run.'

'Well,' the girl said thoughtfully, 'I ain't sayin' I couldn't use that kinda money. Pup spent most what he got on booze. But what makes yuh so sure yuh could hold up a bank an' get away with it? They got hombres in jail right now, as figgered like yuh, to pick up some fast dollars!'

Frank glanced up at the westering sun. It was as yet little after mid-afternoon, but he still had plenty of talking to do, if he were going to sell his idea to this strange, hard-case girl.

'Maybe, it's not so smart, stayin' here an' talkin',' he answered. 'There's a place I know near Lobo Cañon where we ain't likely to be interrupted. Are you willing to hear the details?'

She reached a decision quickly. 'Don't reckon I got anything to lose listenin'. You rid ahaid. I'll follow in the wagon...'

Frank reined in Dave's horse at the stage road and put his glance from left to right before crossing over and beckoning the wagon up.

Less than a mile away lay a deep, but shallow-sided arroyo, so formed amidst surrounding boulder and scrub, that even from near at hand, it was scarcely visible.

It was to this natural hiding-place that Hervey directed the girl with her team and wagon. He watched her capable handling of the vehicle as she ran it over the stony ground, hauled up sharply and slammed on the brake.

She remained on the seat, arms folded across her knees, waiting for the boy's story.

Frank had decided he had little option but to trust her, if he was going to propose a partnership. That meant giving his name, with no attempt at an alias and squarely answering any questions she might put. Maybe he would not divulge the actual place until certain of her support.

He said: 'I'm Frank Hervey. My brother Dave and me run a section over to Spanish Creek, south of Crooked River.'

'I'm Emma. That's what Pup allus said. Reckon he never bothered over any second name. But, this brother o' yours–?'

Frank waved a hand. 'You don't haveta worry over Dave or Ma. Way I've got this thing worked out, it's a cinch.'

He went on to explain how he intended to provide himself with an alibi and how, once they had procured good horses, the animals could be 'disguised'.

Emma gave a snort of derision. 'how kin yuh "disguise" a hoss when its colour an' markin's is a dead giveaway?'

'Spirit dye! An' I know just the place to get it, where the store-keeper ain't likely to identify me, on account of his eyesight's real bad. He can't see clearly above a yard. Another thing, Emma. We both got black hair but by the time we're ready to pull this off we'll be blond! We won't be in town long enough for anyone to pay us close attention. We ride up this side-street, you stay put, holdin' my hoss an' I slip into the bank. No more'n three-four yards to walk. We can be away before anyone knows what's hap-pened–'

'An' where do we ride to, when we find an armed posse breathin' down our necks?'

Frank grinned. 'Lobo Cañon!'

46

Emma drew her dark brows together. 'Ain't travelled much over this part, but seems to me I heerd there wasn't nothin' but box cañons–'

'That's what they all think. Me, I know different, because I ridden clear through to timber an' brush the other side!'

Emma placed one booted foot on the footboard in front of her.

'Reckoned all along, yuh bin figgerin' on me supplyin' the guns. Wal, I guess that's easy, but what of hosses? Them Morgans is powerful built, fer sure, but they ain't fast enough fer our game–'

'If you was to trade them and the wagon,' Hervey put in quickly, 'we could have the finest hoss flesh in the county. You sure won't be needin' a wagon now. Both of us has gotta travel light and fast–'

'Seems like I'm puttin' up a helluva lot, and yuh! Why, yuh only got an idea–!'

'An idea that's going to make us both rich,' Frank said eagerly, leaning forward in the swaddle and laying a hand on her arm. 'Sure, I'm askin' a lot, mebbe it seems,' he argued, 'but this thing's foolproof! Wey Blessiter's bank is sure askin' to be busted and neither Herb Lack, nor yet Will Fiedler, are the hombres to stop us. You pull this with me, Emma, and mebbe other jobs I got lined up and you'll be rich in a few months, far beyond anything you ever figured!'

47

'So! It's the one-horse town o' Wildcat yuh picked on, Frank! I remember, Pup an' me came through 'bout a coupla years back. We see the name o' Blessiter then!'

Frank nodded. He hadn't intended to say quite so much, but the cat was out of the bag now so he pressed forward with all his arguments and promises.

'Soon, I got to be hittin' the breeze,' he finished, glancing towards the west. 'You come with me, Emma, you won't be regrettin' things!'

She looked him over with her hard unwinking stare, for all her tender years, seeing him through a woman's eyes, his brashness, his weaknesses, his vacillatory nature. But seeing also something of the almost fanatical resolve which was driving him now and might well go on driving him to the goal of his ambitions.

'Yuh made a deal, Hervey,' she said at last. 'I know a hoss trader forty miles clear o' here. He will fix me with hosses like yuh ain't never seen. Roans or sorrels, I guess, so yuh kin stain them black. That's what yuh was fixin' to do, wasn't it?

'Mebbe I will git clothes fer the both of us too. Just one small thing, Frank. Yuh forgit to mention a percentage!'

'I wouldn't insult you with anything less than fifty-fifty,' Frank cooed as Emma smiled up into his eyes...

By pushing Dave's roan hard, and by making use of every cut-off, Frank was able to reach Caprock by late afternoon.

It was a satisfied young man who made his simple purchases, quickly and unobtrusively. Not that he had anything to hide at the moment. It was more a case of getting into character, practising little touches such as buying quickly when the assistant's attention was centred on someone else. Frank made it into something of a game covertly observing other folk, whilst contriving to keep himself well in the background.

He felt he could afford now to spend the money Dave had given him. Yet he took care that both the shirt and hat he selected were of a dark indeterminate shade and design and costing no more than a few dollars.

Carefully, he stowed the new shirt into the *alforja* pouch on Dave's saddle, along with the Colt's six-gun and box of shells which Emma had given him before leaving. The ancient hat which perforce had served him since Pa's death, he flung on to the nearest trash pile.

Luck seemed to be favouring him with a vengeance now, for he spotted a pair of worn down half-boots in the windows of a store and repair shop. Some waddy had probably brought them in for repair at one time and had never shown up to claim them and now they were price-tagged at three dollars fifty.

Frank Hervey had no doubts but that Lady Luck was riding at his stirrup. He knew exactly how much money was left in his right-hand pants' pocket. Exactly three dollars fifty!

Again, he managed to efface himself with commendable skill, laying the money on the counter and taking the boots almost before the proprietor had the chance to study him or pass the time of day.

He used a rawhide strip from the saddle to tie the boots together, before stuffing them inside his shirt.

Much as he would have liked to discard his square-toed brogans in favour of these, he knew better than to fall for the temptation. The boots would have to be safely and secretly stashed someplace near home, along with the gun and ammunition. It would be fatal to try smuggling them into the house under Dave's eagle eye!

The sun was down, but a near full moon rode the clear evening sky and Frank was able to make good time on his homeward journey. Whatever else, the roan had stamina to spare and responded well to every demand.

Long before the Hervey house lights winked into view, the youngster had selected the exact spot where he intended caching boots, gun and ammunition.

He splashed through Spanish Creek and dismounted, moving unerringly in the moonlit night to a cairn of stones which lay along the bank at a safe distance from the water's edge.

It was only the work of a few moments to transfer boots, gun and box of shells to their hiding-place, afterwards replacing the uppermost stones in their original position.

Grinning to himself, Frank rode towards the house as Dave opened the door and stepped out into the yard.

'You all right, Frank?'

'Sure. Why not? Even Cinderella was allowed out 'till twelve, wasn't she?'

'It's okay, Frank,' Dave said quietly. 'I didn't mean it that way. Want me to put up the roan?'

Frank was too pleased with recent events to allow irritation to ride him, moreover he had no intention of quarrelling with Dave now.

He smiled down from the saddle. 'You tell Ma to dish up the grub, Dave. I been out ridin', least I can do is care for yore hoss!'

Dave nodded and turned back into the house, a warm glow inside him. It was good to realize that Frank was at last beginning to accept some responsibility. But it went deeper than that. He was developing a new willingness for things, or so it seemed to

Dave, and a chore done voluntarily was worth a dozen executed merely because of orders!

Frank was in fine fettle when he came in and joined the others at the board. He sniffed the food appreciatively and grinned. 'Why'm I allus hungry? Mebbe you don't feed us right, Ma! Say, we got Hatchet beef again for supper?'

Ma and Dave both laughed. 'Better not let Walt hear you makin' jokes like that, Frank!' Ma exclaimed, wiping tears from her eyes. 'This is best Hervey beef, nearly the last, too, of the crittur Dave killed last month.'

'That reminds me–' Dave began, and stopped short as his glance fell on Frank's hat where it hung on the wall antlers.

'So you *did* get a new hat, Frank! Guess I didn't notice out there in the yard–'

'Sure *and* a shirt. It's over there. Nothing fancy. Them stores in Caprock sure ask a lot of *dinero* for their goods.' He was secretly pleased that Dave especially had not noticed the dark brown stetson on his head. It augured well for the future when certain folk might be called on to give detailed descriptions of two bank robbers mounted on black horses.

'Poor Frank!' Ma said, a hint of sadness in her eyes. 'You sure needed them things, and others as well. You'd both be wearing good clothes if only we could stretch the money out, some way.'

Frank busied himself with his food and merely nodded. *There's going to be plenty* dinero *presently,* he thought, *but I won't be able to share it!*

Dave said: 'It's time I trailed a few head up to Caprock, Ma. We got a few good three-year-olds'll fetch a fair price once they're cut out and delivered to Sy Blacklock. But I still got some more sowin' to finish and there's the wagon shed door still not made—'

'I ain't so good on crops an' carpentry, Dave,' Frank said, pushing aside his empty plate, 'but I'll round up the stuff for you, fust thing tomorrow, if you want. Come Monday, you can drive 'em to Caprock.'

'That's fair enough, Frank,' Dave nodded. 'I know you hate sod-bustin' anyway. You cut out ten-twelve steers with the most tallow on them. I figure we can just about manage that number, now most of the cow critturs has dropped their calves.'

'All right,' Frank said. He accepted the cup of coffee from Ma and stirred vigorously, before taking the hot liquid down in a series of gulps.

'Guess I'll turn in now,' he announced, rising from his chair. 'Had a long day an' I gotta be up early.'

He kissed Ma lightly on the cheek and flicked a finger at Dave. He picked up the folded shirt, opened the door leading to his tiny room and shut it quietly behind him.

Once inside, he gazed at the plain, greyish-coloured shirt, seeing it, not as a drab workaday garment, but as a kind of talisman which, like the boots and the gun cached out there on the creek, would enable him to rise up from the dirt and ride the same kind of richly-paved road as folks like Walt Dillon and the Blessiters...

CHAPTER 4

AT SPERRY'S TRADING POST

Dave sat atop the small pole corral, built himself a smoke and gazed at the twelve head of cattle which Frank had rounded up yesterday.

Over to Crooked River the dawn mists were slowly rising and at this early hour Dave was glad of the brush jacket he wore.

The kid had made a good job of hazing the small trail herd, he thought. Only a dozen, true, but it wasn't always easy even for a cow-wrassler to pick exactly the right beasts, chase them around and drive them along in a close, tight bunch.

Dave had been over to inspect the bedded down cattle and had admitted to himself that his own selection would have been no different. Each animal, bearing the 'J.H.' brand and the single earmark which Pa had devised, was sleek and in good shape. Likely to fetch best part of forty dollars, maybe, on the present rising market.

Dave wondered whether some of them might have wandered over on to Hatchet range and had been feeding themselves on Walt's grass, more nutritious and succulent than the sparse stretches along the Creek on Hervey land. If so, Frank hadn't said. He had brought them in last evening, just before dark and it was obvious that the boy had spared neither himself nor his mount. Both had been sweat- and dusk-caked and weary, yet Frank had refrained from his usual grumbles, had insisted on tending and feeding the cow-pony. Immediately after supper, he had quietly slipped off to bed.

And, because of this subtle change for the good in the kid's attitude, Dave found himself turning once again to the dream he had always held in back of his mind. A dream which, because of the everyday pressure of existence, was so seldom allowed to emerge into the light.

Dave Hervey was nothing if not practical and, unlike Pa, he understood the futility of chasing moonbeams. There was precious little time, ever, to sit down and think up ways and means of how to build up a herd or how to find rangeland for the taking. Apart from that, Frank had needed a watchful eye, right from the moment of Pa's death. Dave had had to anticipate his excuses, his alibis and the general short measure which the boy accorded most chores about the homestead.

Now, however, it looked like Frank was finding his level, settling in to the scheme of things and swimming with the tide instead of against it. And for this, Dave felt absurdly grateful.

He began to toy with the proposition Walt Dillon had made on Saturday. Not a real, cut-and-dried proposition, but something more than just a hint. Casually dropped words about paying seven dollars an acre – what had Dillon worked it out as? Over two thousand dollars!

Dave ground out the cigarette as Ma called from the doorway. 'Come and eat, Dave! Bacon's spoilin'!'

He smiled gently. Well, whatever he might plan it would only be gone into with Ma's full agreement. Hervey could not imagine himself going against her wishes.

His mind switched back to Dillon. Three-twenty acres at seven bucks an acre was – two thousand two hundred and forty dollars!

For the first time, Dave let the weight of that figure sink deep down into his brain...

The sun was gilding the eastern sky when Hervey put the roan to the creek and began pushing the now bawling, protesting cattle northwards.

He had to use all the tricks he knew to keep the beasts from fanning out, constantly switching from point and flank positions on either side, using a coiled lariat on bobbing rumps.

As he sweated, Dave realized it would have been a sight easier to have brought Frank along, even though the kid had earned himself a day's rest. After all, Frank had hazed the critturs single-handed, pushed them down from somewhere near Hatchet's eastern boundary, clear down to Spanish Creek. *Maybe he's got more cowman in him than I figured,* Dave thought, wiping dust and sweat from his face.

Once the small herd was clear of grassland, it moved along in a more compact bunch, making Dave's task comparatively easy.

Before noon, he was swinging the bunch along the cattle trail which curved around the trail town of Caprock. On a level stretch some half-mile north of the town were the loading pens and spur track and Dave wasted no time in searching out Sy Blacklock and obtaining the surprisingly good average of thirty-nine dollars fifty per head.

From Sy's talk, and the general indications

in Caprock, Dave deduced that once again, after the disastrous crash three years back, beef prices were soaring to a new high. Even small ranchers who could deliver quantities of fat steers to any of the dozens of shipping points, were pretty sure to show a big profit.

Dave spent a couple of hours moving round the town, exchanging talk with the few folk he knew and making one or two small purchases including a present for Ma, whose birthday it was next Sunday.

After careful deliberation, he had decided on a fine-looking brass table-lamp. True, it was not a particularly *personal* sort of present, but the kind from which others benefited as much, or more, than the recipient. Dave's practical nature could not resist an article so useful, bearing in mind also that it was marked down on account of a dent in the base. But it wasn't too notice-able, and Dave reckoned Ma would be as pleased with it as if she'd had a new dress. Nearly as pleased, anyway.

He wrapped the bulky package in his blankets and retied the roll securely to the saddle cantle.

It was only when he was some three miles out of Caprock, on the way home, that he discovered he was out of tobacco and papers. Well, it would be quicker to turn south-west a little and make for Sperry's Trading Post, than to turn around and return to Caprock.

Aaron Sperry had built the fort-like 'dobe building in his earlier days and had usually managed to freight in his own supplies, even throughout periods of Indian uprisings. But, sometime during his middle life, Sperry had been hit by a musket shot, the ball creasing his forehead, slightly above the brows. In some way, the injury had caused his eyesight to deteriorate rapidly and now, at sixty, it was difficult for him to see clearly beyond a few feet.

But Aaron Sperry had never permitted the disability to get him down. He was usually cheerful, possessed a sharp, dry humour and when the mood took him, would converse freely and authoritatively on politics, literature, in fact, most any subject which might be broached.

Dave liked the oldster and was glad now that he had forgotten to buy tobacco in Caprock. He liked a chat with Sperry and decided now that in future he would patronize the trader for those smaller items which he needed and which the man stocked.

Dave was only mildly surprised to see a Hatchet pony tied outside the 'dobe building. He knew Hatchet riders often dropped in here on those occasions when time would not allow a trip to Wildcat or Caprock.

He tied the roan and moved with his normally quiet tread through the open doorway. He stood stock-still for a second or two, taking in the sight which met his angry, astonished gaze.

For one thing, there was no sign of Aaron himself. Instead, Dave caught a glimpse of the most beautiful girl he had ever seen. Only a glimpse, for she was almost completely screened from his view by the broad back of the Hatchet foreman, Munro Gucht.

Even in the fleeting glance Dave had, he experienced no difficulty in recognizing Gucht's solid width, the inevitable scarlet shirt and blue pants tucked into fancy, long-spurred boots.

Whoever the girl was, it was pretty evident that she more than bitterly resented Munro Gucht's attentions. She stood backed against shelves of canned and dry goods, her shapely body pressed hard against Sperry's merchandise. Fury blazed in her eyes and reflected itself in the half-defiant, half-scared stance.

One sleeve had been torn, ripping the neck-line of her green dress to expose a softly rounded shoulder. Her sorrel hair had shaken free of pins and ribbons and poured down on to her shoulders and breast, like a stream of shimmering molten copper.

At the moment, Gucht's big hands were resting lightly on his hips as he continued to watch the girl, pinning her with his gaze to the stacked wall a yard or so away.

He must have heard the soft scrape of boots on the dirt floor even though he had failed to catch the sound of hoofbeats, earlier. His head swung round, bright glance moving over Dave Hervey with an expression of mingled hostility and contempt.

'Seems like the lady don't care for your kind of – talk, Munro,' Dave drawled. His first hot anger had receded now, leaving him cool and calm despite the fact that he was by no means standing on sure ground.

He was interfering in something between a man he knew and disliked, and a lovely girl who was a complete stranger to him. More than that, Munro Gucht was a salty kind of hombre, big enough, for the most part, to fight his own battles. He could be downright mean when he had been drinking and, from the look of him, Dave decided that Hatchet's ramrod had taken more than a few drinks already.

Those things combined might well have been sufficient to cause even a man of Dave's calibre to refrain from sticking his chin out. And, there was also the fact that whereas none of the Herveys had ever been known to tote a gun, Munro Gucht, in common with all Dillon's hands, consistently wore a pearl-handled Colt's .44. Dave, like many others in Crooked River Valley, had long suspected that it had been this same gun, handled by this same man, which had ended the life of Rosita Morales!

'What I say to Miss Sperry, an' how I say it, ain't any of your dam' business, Hervey!' Gucht sneered. 'But then mebbe it's the preacher blood in you. Better save your talk for that kid brother–'

'What exactly do you mean?' Dave's voice was tight with apprehension.

Munro Gucht lifted broad shoulders in a faint, half-disinterested shrug.

'Don't kid me you don't know Frank's hot for Pearl Gallina! Only trouble is,' the Hatchet man laughed, 'he ain't man enough, nor well-lined enough, to take her from Gil Blessiter!'

Dave's brain raced. He didn't quite know what Gucht was talking about, but it looked as though Frank, like a fool greenhorn, had somehow gotten entangled with Max Cassen's voluptuous singer.

'We'll leave Frank out of it, right now, Munro,' Hervey said through his teeth. 'Mebbe I'd have left you alone now, if Miss Sperry had given me the word. But I ain't passin' over any insult to Ma–'

'You better go while you got the chance, mister, whoever you are! Like Munro said, 'it's none of your business, and–'

'You heard what the lady said,' Gucht smiled, stroking his downswept moustache with thick finger-tips. 'On your way Hervey, while you're still in one piece!'

Dave's narrowed glance swept across to the girl and back to Gucht. If he had ever seen fear, a well as angry scorn channelled into a person's expression, he saw it now in the Sperry girl's wide-open eyes; in the quick intake of her breath and in the very attitude she held with such complete rigidity.

Who does she figure she's kidding? he thought. *She's in a corner, yet she tells me to ride on!*

He said thinly: 'I'm waitin' for you to apologize, Munro, else you'll be leavin' here on a shutter!'

Surprise widened Gucht's thick-lidded eyes. Then for the first time since Dave's entry, anger stained the man's sunburned cheeks a dull crimson. For a moment or two he remained quite still, returning Hervey's cold stare.

Dave took a slow step forward, arms swinging loosely at his sides, big hands loosely balled into fists.

Gucht's answering action was a studied insult in itself. Instead of shaping up to the man a dozen or so paces away, he let his hand drop to the gun at his hip. He must have had a tall opinion of himself – and of his standing in the Valley – to have been so supremely unworried by the Law's reaction. Even the Herb Lacks of the frontier could scarcely shrug away the blatant shooting of an unarmed man. Maybe he was confident too, that the girl could be disregarded as a witness.

Dave saw the gun leap from leather and coiled himself to the tension of a compressed steel spring.

At the precise moment that Gucht's forefinger pulled on the trigger, Dave unleashed himself in a headlong dive at the Hatchet foreman's legs.

Gun-roar shattered the silence and Hervey felt the air whip up as the slug screamed past his head. The muzzle flash momentarily blinded him, but already his long arms had coiled around Gucht's knees, sending both men crashing to the floor with violent impact.

The smoking gun dropped from Gucht's right hand as he sought to obtain a choking grip on Dave's throat.

But Hervey's neck was steel-corded. His own hands came up to grasp the ramrod's thick wrists in an iron-band grip that tore the man's clawing fingers from their hold. But Gucht managed to wrench one hand free and aim a savage blow at Dave's face. It lacked the force Gucht could have given it, had he been on his feet, but it was still powered by the considerable strength of the man's forearm muscles.

Dave's head snapped back and a long cut opened up on his cheek-bone. Momentarily his grip slackened and with a sharp twist of his body, Gucht rolled out from under Hervey's legs.

He was on his feet in an instant, almost before Dave had risen himself. Knotted fists pounded against Hervey's ribs with hammer force. Gucht had seized the slight advantage which had offered and was relentlessly exploiting it to the full.

But it was his turn now to suffer a reverse. As he stepped back to throw a right-hand hook to Dave's out-thrust jaw, his boot came down on the gun still lying on the dirt floor. Gucht's high-heel slipped off the smooth metal, causing him to stagger back off-balance.

For all the pummelling he had received, Hervey was by no means whipped. Like Gucht earlier on, Dave seized his chance and snaked out a vicious left to the ramrod's unguarded jaw. There was plenty of force behind the blow. It caused the man's head to jerk back sharply and for the space of a few seconds his widespread legs sagged at the knees.

As Dave drove in with hard, right and left punches, the girl moved for the first time. Like quicksilver she darted forward, hand diving down and catching up the pearl-handled gun. She was almost knocked over as Dave staggered back from a tremendous blow over the heart.

He gulped down air and shook his head, dimly aware of the mingling of blood and sweat on his face.

But Munro Gucht was in worse shape. Though both men were fairly evenly matched, the Hatchet man was the heavier of the two. His body was just beginning to accumulate surplus flesh much in the way Walt Dillon had done already.

Dave's vision cleared and he saw that Gucht's barrel-chest was heaving with his efforts. His big, handsome face was rapidly becoming a patchwork affair with yellow-blue discolorations appearing where Dave's hard-boned knuckles had struck. Blood oozed from Gucht's nose, trickling down and congealing on the sagging, longhorn moustache. Dave refilled his lungs with air and stepped forward, guard wide open. If Gucht had been in better shape, he might well have decided the fight in his favour there and then.

As it was, his arms lifted only with the greatest difficulty and pain. He was just that mite slower than his adversary, and Hervey packed most of his remaining strength into a shattering blow that landed on the point of the Hatchet man's chin.

Gucht fell back, tried to save himself, but lacked the necessary co-ordination and strength. He crashed down on to the hard-packed floor and lay there, eyes closed and breath coming in short, rasping gasps.

Dave moved back groggily, stood there breathing deeply and waiting until his legs felt strong enough to carry him.

Slowly he untied the polka-dot bandana from his neck and painfully began to wipe face, neck and hands.

He turned his head and looked at the girl, seeing the fear gone from her eyes replaced by an expression of tender concern.

'Are – are you all right, mister–?'

He grinned and, looking at her rescuer, Sorrel Sperry thought she had never seen such an engaging smile, even though the man's face was bruised and bloody.

'I'll get you some hot water and salves,' she said, suddenly becoming conscious of the gun's weight on her arm.

Dave moved stiffly over to where she stood by the disarranged counter. He held out a hand and she dropped Gucht's gun on to it.

She watched him eject the spent cartridge and the five live shells. The latter he placed carefully on the counter. 'Next time Gucht calls,' Dave smiled, 'mebbe you'll give 'em back to him. It might kinda remind him to go more careful in the future.'

'More likely it'll remind him that a certain

man called – Hervey, isn't it? – called his bluff and thrashed him in front of a woman who didn't want any interference!'

Dave moved his glance over to where Gucht lay. The man stirred slightly but he would cause no more trouble this day.

'Why?' Dave asked simply, returning his attention to the girl.

'I – I guess I figured he would beat you up, maybe kill you – I didn't want an innocent bystander to–'

'Since when did old Aaron have a daughter hidden away someplace?' Dave said switching the conversation.

Looking at the girl now, he could see little, if any, resemblance in features and colouring to the old trader. Her hair, still unpinned and flowing about her shoulders, was as near the colour of a horse-chestnut as made no never-mind. Eyes were more green than grey and fringed with long, dark lashes. The mobile lips were redder than those of any woman in Wildcat, except Pearl Gallina's; but they were not so obvious looking as Pearl's.

'Aaron's my uncle,' she explained. 'I only just arrived yesterday from Albuquerque on a vacation. I offered to look after the post while Uncle drove to Stella. Guess I don't seem to have made a success of it,' she smiled, surveying the fallen cans and spilled goods scattered around.

Dave smiled. 'Mebbe you've even lost a valuable customer!'

She pushed away from the counter. 'Stay there while I get that hot water, Mr Hervey. Time we are gossiping, those cuts and bruises sure aren't likely to improve.'

Dave turned, moved across to Gucht now sitting up and holding his jaw in one blood-stained hand. He bent down, gripped the foreman's arms and hauled him upright. Gucht swayed a little but contrived to maintain his balance. His hate-filled gaze touched Hervey like a burning brand, as Dave slid the Colt's gun back into its holster.

The Hatchet man's battered lips drew back from his teeth in a venomous snarl. 'You made a big mistake, hornin' in–'

'Climb aboard, Munro, an' start ridin',' Hervey said softly and stepped across to the open door.

He took his time, walking with measured tread until he reached Dave. He stopped then and stood regarding the other for a full half minute, a bitter, implacable light shining in his dark eyes.

Dave waited, thumbs hooked into belt, reading the naked warning in Gucht's eyes, until the ramrod finally stepped outside and laboriously hauled himself into the saddle.

CHAPTER 5

DAVE SUPPLIES AN ANSWER

Sorrel dropped the blood-stained cloth into the bowl, gently dabbed at Hervey's face with a towel and applied salves to cuts and abrasions.

'I guess I haven't even thanked you, Mr Hervey, for – for coming to my help like you did. I was real scared–'

'What happened in the beginning?' Dave pulled out his Durham sack and scowled down at the few dry fragments.

Immediately, Sorrel Sperry placed a jar of tobacco on the counter at his elbow.

'There's not a lot to it. He rode up mebbe a half-hour or so before you did. Bought a few things, talking most of the time while I served him. Likely he figured he was paying me some real nice compliments!

'Well, I guess I was anxious not to lose my first customer. After all, Aaron can't make much money here, or so it seems to me. Then Gucht started getting bolder. He had told me his name and who he was and stupidly, perhaps, I gave him my name, told him who I was, where I came from, that kinda thing.

'He – he tried to kiss me – caught hold of my arms. There was a struggle and in wrenching free, my dress got torn. By then I'd smelled the liquor on his breath and guessed he had been drinkin' mebbe heavily. I was getting pretty scared. It sure was a relief when you came in though I began to realize it was goin' to take a very strong man to – subdue Mr Munro Gucht!'

'Munro can be tough an' right mean when he likes,' Dave informed. 'He's range-boss for Walt Dillon's spread an' rods it over near a dozen riders. They're a rough bunch, an' now and again one or other of 'em breaks out. I guess it was Munro's turn this time!'

'You had better watch out, Mr Hervey. I feel sure he's likely fixin' to take his revenge–'

'I feel kinda sure of that myself,' Dave smiled. 'But hadn't we oughta set this place to rights before Aaron gets back?'

Sorrel smiled. 'He won't be back until around dusk, but I'd be might grateful for your help again, Mr–'

'The first name's "Dave",' he told her, reaching down and starting to pick up the scattered goods...

Frank had arranged to meet Emma at the hidden arroyo, as soon after noon on Wednesday as possible.

He knew that so far, he had played his

71

cards well, that his stock stood unusually high both with Dave and Ma. But he still had to find some sure-fire excuse for getting away from the section. Some chore which he could do well enough to satisfy Dave, but which would not interfere with his vital rendezvous with Emma!

He straightened up from the back-breaking chore of hoeing, a task which he had voluntarily undertaken as much to give himself a chance to work things out, as to please his elder brother.

Ma was in the house someplace and Dave was sowing an alfalfa patch. Frank could slack off somewhat without risking Dave's disapproval.

An eagerness stirred in Hervey today, the same kind of effervescent bubbling he had experienced last Saturday on the drive home from town. It was scarcely necessary to remind himself that today was Wednesday and that somehow he had to get away before noon, *to reassure himself that the dark-haired girl had not changed her mind!*

Suppose, he thought for the hundredth time, she got scared after she thought it over? Maybe she's not so tough as I figured her! Or maybe she's fixin' to do the same kind of job on her own, an' rake in the whole pot!

Frank wiped the sweat from his face and shifted the hoe back to his right hand. For the first time since wakening this morning, the pulsating excitement in him drained away. For perhaps the first time he began to realize that the whole scheme, its very existence as well as potential success, lay in the hands of the strange, wild-looking creature he had met up with for the first time, four days ago.

In this sudden, defeatist mood he had a mental picture of her driving steadily on, the Morgans still hitched to the smart wagon, and contempt etched in every line of her dark-skinned face, for the wild scheme she had listened to from some half-crazy kid!

Frank swallowed, feeling his tongue and mouth go dry. With an effort, he switched his thoughts away from the gloomy channel into which he had allowed them to drift.

At least, even in his most pessimistic frame of mind, he could not deny that so far everything had worked out perfectly. Events had shaped themselves to his plans with the precision of expertly chiselled joints. There was no denying it, and he even gave a tight smile as he thought back on Sunday, when, acting on a blind hunch, he had combined the work of cutting out the cattle with the job of procuring the jars of black stain!

At first, the idea had not occurred to him. Only later, when he had started in combing the breaks along Crooked River for a dozen likely steers, had he decided to seize this opportunity with both hands.

From the first, he had selected Sperry's Trading Post as the best place to buy what he needed.

The old man was dam' near blind anyway, and wouldn't be likely to recognize him, even though both Dave and himself occasionally traded there.

In any case, Sperry's testimony wouldn't ever be good for much in a court of law, on account of everyone knew he couldn't see so well. And, to have bought ammonia and black spirit stain in Wildcat or Caprock or even Stella, would have been plumb foolish for sure!

Besides, the trading post was much nearer, and yet tucked away on a now unfrequented trail. Thus Frank had killed the two birds with one stone; had wellnigh cleared himself out of *dinero* in purchasing the stuff he needed from old Aaron.

He had cached the bottles along with the boots and gun under the cairn of rocks, after having sweated blood to cut-out and haze the gather for Dave.

It was not until Dave had returned from driving the herd to Caprock, that Frank fully appreciated just how clever, or lucky, he had been in making his purchases *no more than a few hours before Aaron's niece had shown up!*

He ran the hoe between two rows of

74

potatoes, recalling Ma's consternation to mind when she had first glimpsed Dave's battered face!

Frank had experienced conflicting emotions as he and Ma had listened to Dave's terse account. Both admiration and a resentful kind of envy had touched him for a while. After all, Dave *was* a Hervey and Munro Gucht a rough and dangerous man!

Even though Dave had given no more than the barest outline of his tangle with the Hatchet foreman, it was clear he must have beaten Gucht pretty conclusively.

But the girl whom Dave had called Sorrel, was the one who interested Frank most. Or rather, *it was her presence at the trading post,* revealed through Dave's story, which had caused Frank to be somewhat more than merely *interested.*

If he had delayed buying the stain and the bleach even by a few hours, most likely he would have come face to face with this girl. Thus, unless he were to take a big risk, he would have been forced to buy the stuff somewhere else. It was one thing to rely on an old man's near blindness when it came down to a question of identity; it was something quite different to be confronted by someone very much in possession of all their faculties. Someone who would likely make a first-class witness for the prosecution!

Frank had sweated at the very thought. But later, his old confidence had returned and thereafter he had continued to regard his 'escape' as a good omen...

Now, the immediate problem was how to meet Emma. Time was running by. Already it was approaching the forenoon and suddenly Frank grinned widely, vaguely wondering why he had not thought of so simple a solution before.

There was still the other obstacle to overcome. How could he hold up Blessiter's bank next Saturday and at the same time, make Ma and Dave believe he was some place miles away from Wildcat? Not that either of them would suspect him of complicity in the robbery. The thought would not enter their minds. But, it would be as well to have an unshakeable alibi which could be casually offered in the event of any later questioning by Sheriff Lack and Deputy Will Fiedler!

Oddly, it was Dave himself who furnished part of the answer. And, by the time Frank had expanded the idea, it became a *complete* answer!

In spite of his intense preoccupation Frank had made a passable job of the hoeing. When Dave appeared suddenly from the house and approached the potato patch, he nodded appreciatively at the work.

'Got somethin' to show you, Frank. It's in the wagon-shed—'

Mystified, Frank gazed at Dave, wondering what it was all about and suddenly feeling a vague unease.

But Dave, laughing now, gripped his arm, leading him towards the outbuildings. At least Frank thought, whatever it was it had the advantage of taking him away from the hateful chore of hoeing, and his brother was sure in a good mood.

He followed Dave into the shed and watched curiously as the latter pulled several empty sacks and bundles of straw from the corner and dived a hand down into the large box which now stood revealed. Still considerably puzzled, Frank gazed at the shaded table lamp which his brother was holding up for inspection.

'What d'you think of that, Frank?' He smiled. 'Sure looks a beauty, don't she? I've cleaned an' rubbed it once already. A few more good polishes an' it will shine like gold!'

'Sure, it's fine! But what's the uproar about? Mebbe we *can* use a new lamp, sure is time, but why the excitement an' – an' secrecy?'

Dave's bruised face registered good-natured disgust as he carefully replaced the lamp and redraped the box with the straw and wheat sacks.

He sighed and thrust his hands deep into trouser pockets.

'You've done forgot again, Frank! Every year I got to remind you that Ma's birthday falls on May twenty-six–'

A light burst on Frank then and he grinned sheepishly. 'It ain't that I forgot, Dave–'

Frank knew himself to be lying, and so did Dave. But he was grinning widely at the 'guilty' expression on his kid brother's face and, suddenly, both of them were laughing fit to bust!

It was always the same, every year, and Frank no longer bothered to think up a good excuse for his failing.

The episode had momentarily caused Frank's problem to slip from his mind and he now started to select the words most calculated to produce Dave's ready agreement to the idea. Dave, still smiling a little, stepped outside the shed and began rolling a cigarette.

Frank moved to join him and all at once the solution to his problem was right there, staring him in the face!

'I guess I allus did forget anniversaries! Ma's, yours, even my own. Mebbe I ain't got a memory for dates but now you've mentioned it – there was somethin' I saw in Caprock last Saturday, when I bought the shirt an' hat–' Frank paused, recollecting the small French clock he had idly noticed in the window of a jewellery store.

'It might mean borrowing a few bucks from you, Dave,' he continued, 'but there was a fella in Caprock I ain't set eyes on for mebbe more'n a year. Last time I met him he was down on his luck an' I kinda staked him–'

'How–'

'Oh, only a few dollars I'd gotten saved up,' Frank explained blandly. 'Anyways, seems like he struck it rich someplace. Swore he'd pay me back with interest. Guess I wasn't goin' to mention it until it had happened!'

Dave laid an arm across his brother's shoulders. This was the kind of talk he liked to hear from Frank. The kid might be un-interested in sod-bustin' to the point of apparent laziness, but he was solid gold deep down inside.

'Your credit's okay with me,' he grinned. 'I'll advance you anything up to twenty-five dollars if that'll cover the price. What is it, anyway?'

'It's my turn for a mystery surprise,' Frank grunted. 'I'll ride into Caprock Saturday, get the present an' look out for the hombre who figgers to show his gratitude in hard cash–'

'Sure, Frank. You do that. Set off right early an' spend the day there. But keep a clear head for Ma's birthday on Sunday.'

Dave was thinking, *the kid will be all right in Caprock; at least he won't be mixing it with Pearl Gallina, if there was any truth in Munro Gucht's suggestion!*

Frank nodded. He was scraping earth from the hoe he still held and glanced up as though suddenly remembering something else.

'Reckon I should've mentioned it before, but at the time I was so dead-beat – an' after that, well, I guess this was somethin' else I jest natcherally forgot!'

'Something serious?'

Frank shook his head. 'No need to start in worryin', Dave. Jest that when I was chasin' them critturs over to Hatchet's boundary on Sunday, I saw what looked like some of our stuff chawin' away on Walt's grass. Not many, mebbe ten twelve or so. Difficult to say at that distance an' there was no time to ride over for a look-see. My hands was full–'

'I know,' Dave nodded. 'You did a swell job cutting out those steers an' pushin' 'em single-handed. But I was goin' to ask you the same thing–'

'Well,' Frank put in quickly. 'I'd sure admire to be ridin' 'stead of hoein'. The potato patch is near enough clear of weeds now. What say I take a *pasear* an' push any them trespassers back? Might save Walt or Gucht gettin' funny!'

'It'd be a great help, Frank. I got plenty to do around here right now. But soon as we're sure all the stuff's back on Spanish Creek, I'd like your help on some brandin'.' Dave's face set into sober lines.

'Mebbe you're right about Walt or Munro gettin' uppity. In his present mood, Gucht wouldn't be above throwing a Hatchet iron on any young stuff he found!'

He moved away and then swung round. 'Better take the buckskin. It'll make the job that much easier.'

Frank nodded, his gaze following Dave as the latter walked back to the house with long, easy strides.

The buckskin was Dave's pride. A trained cow-pony which the Hervey's had bought last fall from a horse-trader travelling through Wildcat. Dave had managed to get it for forty dollars on account it was lame in the off-side foreleg. Otherwise it might have fetched nearer a hundred.

As it was, the outlay had set them back considerably, but Dave had insisted it was a bargain. After all, whilst the roan was good for many more years, it only left the old shaft horse for Frank when both the brothers were needed for cow-punching. It just showed that Dave was a right guy to offer it, even if he was a slave-driver!

Frank had his moment of deep regret then, almost wishing that there was no Ma and no Dave.

I'm sure sorry to do this to you, brother Dave, but I ain't figurin' on wastin' the rest of my life diggin' out weeds an' playin' around with fifty head of nester stock!

I got plans, Dave. Plans which you an' Ma'd figger downright wicked, I guess. But that ain't the way I see it. Some folks has got a sight too much an' don't even rough their hands or bend their backs to git it! But we can work the clock round. An' me! Why, Dave, when I need the price of a drink or a new shirt, I gotta ask you for the cash or borrow it!

But don't fret, Dave. No one's gonna be smart enough to figger it's the Hervey kid who's pullin' these jobs!

Slowly the boyish softness receded from Frank's face leaving it set in lines of vicious determination. He thought back on the story he had told Dave about the man in Caprock who'd struck it rich and was eager to remember those who had helped him. That bit had been an inspiration. He would be able to flash at least some of the money he took from Blessiter's explaining that 'the fella' had *really* struck it rich and had paid out lavishly.

Another thing. Maybe Pearl would change her ideas some when the ragged Hervey kid showed up rigged out like a top-hand. That would sure enough wipe the smile from Gil Blessiter's face!

82

In his mind's eye, Frank saw himself decked out something in the fashion of the Hatchet riders. Even better. More like Munro Gucht with his shiny spurred boots, striped pants and brightly coloured, expensive shirts.

There was a beautifully polished gun in Frank's right hand. Thumb flicked back the knurled hammer as forefinger squeezed the trigger. He felt the acrid bite of gunsmoke in his nostrils, tasted it on his tongue. A tremendous sense of power surged through him...

Frank's gaze focused once more on his immediate surroundings. He glanced up at the sun and saw that the time was only a little short of noon. With an effort, he dragged himself back from the satisfying world of make-believe. Soon, very soon, he told himself, it would be the real thing! Quickly he saddled and bridled the buckskin, flung himself into the saddle and galloped from the yard in a whirl of dust. He didn't want Ma calling him back at the last moment.

There were worse things than riding for a few hours on an empty belly. The fair chance that Emma might not show up would be a sight worse than skipping the noon meal!

Making sure that his actions could not be overlooked from the house, Frank slid from leather, dropped lightly to his feet by the cache.

He wasn't bothering with anything except the gun. This was the opportunity he needed to accustom himself to its balance and weight; maybe the chance to fire it, once he was well clear of Spanish Creek.

With no gun-belt or holster in his possession, Frank thrust the weapon into his waist-band and climbed back into the saddle.

Within the hour, he was approaching the hidden arroyo and shortly he reined in atop a brush-stippled ridge to give the surrounding country a wide-sweeping, careful scrutiny...

CHAPTER 6

RENDEZVOUS

Over to the south-west, on Hatchet land, a few slow-moving dots indicated that some of the hands were out working the cattle. But Frank was not worried that he could be identified or even seen from that distance, particularly as the immediate terrain favoured concealment.

But caution, and an almost animal-like

wariness were becoming second nature to him, and when he finally urged the buckskin to lower ground, it was to begin a slow, circling movement which would bring him to the far end of the arroyo's rim.

It took a full half-hour, riding as he was with infinite caution, to reach a point from where he could peer down to the rock floor of the depression.

Somehow, he was scarcely surprised to find the hide-out completely empty of life. Yet it was impossible to shake off the mood of vicious anger that swept over him at the discovery.

He glanced upwards to the cloud-flecked sky and judged the time as somewhere around one-thirty. Well, it was still not *too* late, he supposed, even though the rendez-vous had been timed for noon or before.

Emma knew well enough that *he* might not be able to make it dead on time. But, Hell! *she* was a free agent! There was nothing to stop her being here on time with the horses, *if she intended coming at all!*

Presently the anger in him slowly gave way to a feeling of morbid defeat. He descended the shallow slope and ground-tied the buckskin, afterwards returning on foot to the rim and selecting a spot that afforded sufficient cover to allow him to watch, without being visible himself.

He squatted there, aware now of the rising

heat from the rocks, cursing softly to himself and wishing fervently that he had some whisky. He had decided to wait until the sun showed three hours past noon. After that, he would have to resign himself to the inevitable, temporarily at least, and then ride hell for leather in search of any strayed Hervey beeves.

But after only a further fifteen minutes, the old restlessness and quick impatience spread through him.

He remembered that he had grabbed the filled canteen from the stable, after saddling the buckskin, and had dropped its looped strap over the saddle-horn; an unthinking, yet instinctive precaution.

Well, a drink of water was better than no drink at all! He rose from the piñon and rock cover and, one foot on the arroyo slope, turned his gaze on to the country north-west.

He stiffened, squinting his eyes against light-glare, focusing on to a spot three-four miles away. He had seen movement along a narrow, stony trail in that first swift glance. Now he shaded his eyes, making a roofed arch with cupped hands and the brim of his stetson.

There were two mounted figures visible now! No! One rider only, leading a spare horse!

In a fever of impatience Frank waited out

the necessary time until the object of his scrutiny could be identified with absolute certainty.

Shortly, he was able to discern that the rider was slim and small, that the horses appeared big. Roans or sorrels by the looks of things. He was pretty sure now, yet a mental reserve held him from immediately acknowledging something which his eager gaze had already identified.

The last doubts, if doubts they had been, evaporated as the girl's features became more easily recognizable.

It was Emma, dam' her! And she had been as good as her word, after all! There had been no need to sweat and stew. She was in this thing with him, right up to the hilt, prepared to ride alongside into a future bright with the shine of gold!

He flourished his hat in a gesture half-excited, half-triumphant and watched her hand lift in acknowledgement.

A little later, Frank found himself gazing up into the girl's hard black eyes in which lay the faintest glitter of sly amusement.

She had discarded the buckskin skirt in favour of waist overalls. Over the dark shirt she wore a calf-hide vest, a common enough garment in cow-country. The stetson was pulled well down over her dark-hued face, and a loosely knotted bandana swathed her bare throat.

Frank had to admit she had selected her clothes with a rare and shrewd judgement, obviously having rejected anything fancy or conspicuous in favour of the more non-descript.

He noticed the same scarred Justins on her feet as those she had worn before, but with the addition of sunflower spurs.

'Mebbe yuh'll know me next time, Frank!'

He pushed back his hat and surveyed her coolly. The former buoyant confidence had returned to lift his spirits skywards.

'I was admirin' the outfit, Emma, not what's inside it!'

She smiled. This was the kind of talk she best understood, and appreciated. From bitter experience she had learned what invariably lay behind the fabric of a man's honeyed words.

'You done well!' Frank had transferred his attention to the roans. Not only were they about the best-looking horses he had ever seen, but serviceable kaks were cinched to both and from the right-hand stirrup fender of each one, the walnut butt of a Winchester carbine protruded.

The girl swung down, trailing the reins. She reached down into the saddle pocket and silently handed Frank a shapeless looking object wrapped in a crimson bandana.

'Well, go ahaid, an' undo it, fer Kansas

Pete's sake, 'stead o' jest a-starin'!'

He didn't like it when her tongue got sharp, but he only nodded, untied the bandana and found himself gaping at a cartridge-studded belt complete with holster.

A sudden gush of warmth and gratitude towards this wild creature swept over him. Here was something else he had always longed for and had never possessed. Yet, she had already supplied him with a Navy Colt's gun which any hombre would be real proud to own. Now she had casually thrown a filled gun-belt at him–

There was a hotness in his eyes and throat. He started to speak and then checked himself sharply. This nomad girl had shown her contemptuous dislike for any kind of emotional exhibitionism and quickly now, Frank realized the necessity for matching her own detached and callous attitude to life in general.

'Thanks, Emma!' He managed a cool smile and buckled the belt around his hips, transferring the gun from waistband to holster and resisting the temptation to try his speed at drawing.

Emma was chewing at a piece of jerky, sharp teeth tearing at it with all the uninhibited savagery of an animal.

'You got everything figured?' she asked, stuffing the last of the meat into her mouth.

She wiped her hands on the seat of her pants and brought her hard gaze back to Frank's face.

From an inner coat pocket, Hervey produced a folded scrap of paper, smoothed it and held it out for the girl's inspection.

'This is Main Street, Emma, an' the cross is Blessiter's. You kin see the side-street, there! We–'

'Where's the Peace Officers' hang out?'

'Sheriff Herb Lack's office is down-street a way. Lack ain't anythin' much to worry over, but he gotta deppity, Will Fiedler–'

'He smart?'

'Fiedler might bear watchin', but if this goes like I planned it, the law ain't goin' to git a look in!

'But to come back. Lack's office is on the same side o' the street as Wey Blessiter's bank–'

'That means, was we lucky, they won't see us at all.'

She pointed with a sunburned finger to a position on the rough plan, beside the cross.

Frank nodded. 'You got it. That's where we pull up an' I head for the bank. Soon as I'm on the boardwalk, you turn the hosses around, back the way we come in.

'Reckon I'll be out in three-four minutes with a flour sack full of cash. Then we hit the breeze, head for this stand of cottonwoods an' double back–'

'But–'

Frank shook his head and grinned.

'They won't know we're doubling back an' heading west on account we'll be travellin' along a dried-up water course. Even if some fools *was* quick enough to take out after us *pronto,* time they savvy which way to ride we'll be screened by a series of ridges here.'

He indicated the area he had marked on the map.

'From there, we're covered most all the way to Lobo Cañon. Once through the cañon, we circle round an' head back here–'

'Here?'

'Why not?' Frank countered. 'Folks don't ever ride this way. No reason to. Ain't any trails that go any place 'ceptin' fer a few cut-offs as lead to Caprock, an' I guess even Lack an' Fiedler don't know them!'

Emma rolled herself a quirly, wiped a match alight and thoughtfully blew smoke down her thin nostrils.

'Why can't we dust it straight back here, 'stead o' trailin' through Lobo Cañon? You said no folks ever come thisaway!'

'Way I see it,' Frank explained, 'Lack's posse'll likely take its time an' look fer tracks. We ride straight back here, mebbe Fiedler *might* nose us out. The other way, any sign we leave, which won't be much anyways, 'll vanish soon as we hit the shale stretches along the cañons.'

Emma nodded. There was a glint of near admiration in her black eyes as she returned her gaze to Hervey's face.

'Whadda we do next?'

He placed a hand on his rumbling belly. 'You got any grub left in your saddle pocket?'

She moved across to the roan, thrusting a hand into the saddle pouch, discovering another slice of jerky and a hunk of stale bread.

Again Frank took care not to indulge in too great a show of gratitude, accepting the tough food with no more than a slight gesture of acknowledgement.

'Soon's we git back here,' he went on, 'we split the *dinero* fifty-fifty, like we agreed. Then we light out fer Caprock where I will have left my own hoss tied on Main Street.'

'Yuh ain't so dumb,' she acknowledged. 'Kinda fixin' yourself with an alibi, I reckon. But *I* ain't figgerin' on ridin' into no town–'

'You don't have to,' Frank returned quickly. 'An' I ain't fool enough to ride into Caprock on a hoss thet mebbe folks'll identify.

'No, Emma. We only ride as far as the outskirts of the town. There's plenty cover around an' you kin travel on any which way you want. I'm gonna snuck in along a side-street an' show myself some, before ridin' out.'

She chewed on that a while, but could see nothing much wrong with the plan except for one thing.

'Yuh said somethin' about stainin' the hosses black–?'

'Sure,' he nodded. 'Come to think of it, mebbe you'd best wait for me outside Caprock. That way, I kin ride with you an' find some quiet spot to scrub them roans back to their natural colour. Even if anyone *did* spot you, they wouldn't ever tie up a girl an' two roans with a coupla bank robbers forkin' blacks!'

'It shore sounds good enough, Frank. When do we throw it? I'm jest about cleaned out!'

He nodded savagely. 'That makes two of us, Emma, but it ain't fer long. You meet me right here at an hour after dawn next Saturday. That's goin' to give us plenty time to paint the hosses, git everythin' ready an' take a roundabout route into Wildcat.

'I'm aimin' to time this hull thing pretty careful. Two o'clock Saturday afternoon is the one time Blessiter's is most likely to be full of *dinero* an' empty of customers. I tell you, Emma, this hour come Saturday we're gonna be playin' poker with greenbacks, 'stead o' cairds!'

'It shore don't seem possible we could slip up,' she said softly...

The next few days were the most exacting that Frank had ever lived through.

For, whilst his mind was busy finalizing and perfecting his scheme, he found it increasingly difficult to concentrate on the normal, mundane chores around the homestead.

That wasn't so bad in itself, but when Dave or Ma spoke to him, he experienced the greatest difficulty in switching his thoughts quickly from future to present.

Once or twice when Ma gave him a worried, yet affectionate glance, he realized he was playing too dangerous a game in allowing his mind to become swamped, to the exclusion of everyday things.

He must guard against attracting undue attention by confining mental exploration of these last-minute details to those times when he worked alone, or better still, when he retired to his own room at night.

Fortunately, Dave was so almighty busy himself, that he appeared not to notice any particular preoccupation on the part of his younger brother. But Ma was a different kettle of fish, Frank thought. It was a bit weird how some women seemed able to know what was in back of a man's mind, especially women like Ma!...

Well, at least, on Wednesday afternoon, he had managed to find some seventeen 'J.H.' critturs unconcernedly using Hatchet graze and had succeeded in turning them back to Spanish Creek, even though it had meant going without grub the best part of the day.

Ma had been a mite concerned over that and only started to relax after Frank had asked for, and received, a third large helping of supper.

He looked up now and grinned, as Ma dished out the noon meal.

'I was jest thinkin' how much supper I ate last night, Dave. First off, Ma was plumb worried on account I missed dinner; next, she started gittin' anxious 'cos I couldn't *stop* eatin'!'

'Figured you might give yourself indigestion, for one thing,' Ma smiled, 'and also, I could see we might be needin' some more beef for today. There ain't goin' to be much left by supper tonight, I'm thinkin'.'

'You think I oughta kill another steer, Ma, or should one of us drive into town an' haul back enough to last over a few days?' Dave suggested.

A sudden, wild idea flashed into Frank's mind. He found himself replying to Dave's question before Ma could make answer.

'I'll go find an old mossy-horn along the brakes, Dave, an' kill it for you. Skin it as well. You sure showed me how to, often enough, but you ain't never let me do it on my lonesome?'

'Think you could?' Dave smiled, pleased

at his brother's enthusiasm.

'Sure I could, Dave Hervey, an' you know it! What about it, Ma? You don't want no butcher's meat, do you?'

'I ain't keen, boys, as you know. Town meat's never so fresh an' the weather's warming up some. Guess it's cheaper, too, if Dave figures we can spare another cow?'

'Not a cow crittur, Ma. We'll have to make do with an old mossy-horn, like Frank says. Reckon you could cut out the oldest lookin' steer, kill an' skin it an' tote it back in the wagon?'

'You bet I could!' Frank grinned. 'I'll start out *pronto*. Remember seein' an old beef crittur when I chased the "trespassers" back off Walt's grass yesterday!'

He was pleased that he now had some hard physical cow-work with which to occupy himself until the evening. Man's work this, was, a sight more so than planting corn or potatoes or alfalfa, and waiting weeks for any results to show.

Besides, this was not just a case of cutting out a 'J.H.' steer and butchering it. There was something more to Frank's idea than that. *He intended pulling down a Hatchet beast, slaughtering and skinning it and burying the tell-tale hide some place until he could sell it safely!*

He recalled then, that after Saturday, he would not have to bother over selling a hide for a few dollars. That kind of money would be chicken feed in comparison with what he *would* have even after dividing the haul equally with Emma!

Still, the whole idea was exciting and the thought of being able to put something over on Hatchet, even though Walt himself wasn't so bad, left Frank with a pleasant feeling of reckless satisfaction.

Dave was walking across the yard as Frank set wagon and team to the open country. He waved a carefree hand and Dave lifted an arm in salute, the wide smile on his lips reaching up to brighten his eyes...

Once he had forded the creek, Frank held the team to a steady trot, now and again glancing down at the .22 rifle at his feet.

He would have preferred trying out the Colt's again, selecting a steer, close-herding it and firing at point-blank range. But he had figured it unwise to stop at the creek and lift the gun from its hiding-place. Dave was wandering around and might spot the stationary vehicle, wonder what had caused him to haul up.

But Emma's gun had reacted perfectly yesterday afternoon and after Frank had gotten used to its kick, he had close-ringed five slugs on a piñon stump at a distance of thirty yards.

The very feel of the carefully balanced weapon had given Frank Hervey a tremendous sense of power. He would have liked nothing better than to spend the rest of the day at target practice. But though he had chosen the spot carefully, he had been scared some of Dillon's hands might be riding near enough to hear the shots and come horning in.

Apart from such possible interruptions, Frank had figured it wouldn't be smart to use up too many shells, and as well, he would have to burn leather if he were to push back the drifting cattle and get back to home before nightfall...

Now that he was again engaged on a chore of his own choosing, he began to relish every moment.

Problems and details concerning the protracted raid on Wildcat's bank sank into the deeper recesses of his mind, giving prior place to the immediate plan now shaping in his head.

He knew a spot farther along the river where most times some of Hatchet's stuff drifted; a place usually devoid of riders except at round-ups.

Two-three times, Frank pulled up to rest the team and to lay his searching gaze over the folds and ridges of Dillon's range. And, by the time he had reached the stretch of grass bottomland, he was reasonably sure there were no Hatchet riders within miles.

He grinned as he spotted a small bunch of

cattle, heads raised now, suspicious, inquiring, at the sound of his approach.

More by chance than design, he had come up to them on a slight head-on breeze and this gave him the time he needed to get close in for a sure shot.

They were on the point of scattering when Frank's rifle barked. At once the small bunch went into a minor stampede, crashing through brush and tall grass in their panic to escape the danger threatening them behind.

With the quick surge of satisfaction which every hunter knows, the boy observed that the big steer he had singled out had dropped, and was wildly threshing its legs.

He leaped down from the wagon, jamming the brake on and quickly tying the reins to the front near-side wheel. This time he tested the wind direction, making sure that the team would not catch the scent of death.

He ran forward and drove a point-blank shot into the steer's brain and without further ado, set to work with his knife in the manner shown him so often by Dave.

CHAPTER 7

KROELLER'S LIFE OR HIS!

It was gruelling, back-aching work for one so unaccustomed to it as Frank Hervey.

Bending over the dead steer all the time and cutting away with his knife, he found it increasingly necessary to pause every so often; to straighten up and ease his aching muscles, and wipe the sweat from face and neck.

But for all his slim build, lacking as he did the muscular bulk of his brother, Frank was wiry enough and, in his present mood, fiercely determined not to be licked by the job now. At the end of nearly two hours' punishing work, the hide lay at his feet in no more than three main pieces.

He took time off to wash up at the river's edge, cleaning blood and muck from his arms, afterwards taking a long pull from the canteen which he had brought along in the wagon.

Anxious as he was to quarter the carcass and load up, he forced himself to rest for a full half-hour and occupied the last few minutes of his self-enforced break period by

100

reloading the deer rifle.

He was leaning against the wagon-side, gun in hand, when one of the team gave a shrill nicker.

There was scarcely time to move his head round before a grating voice sounded from beyond the other side of the wagon.

'Whadda yuh figger yuh're doin' with thet dead steer, sonny? Fixin' to butcher it?'

Frank's gaze swivelled slowly until he found himself staring into the cold eyes of Bart Kroeller, one of Dillon's tougher hands.

He was a wizened little man, appearing small and shrunken even atop the piebald pony. His bristled face was the colour of freshly turned soil and furrowed with a thousand wrinkles.

Frank continued to stare with the fixed fascination of a calf gazing at a mountain lion. For those first few seconds his arm and leg muscles were too stiff with shock and fear for any kind of movement.

Slowly, it seemed to the petrified boy, he absorbed the fact that Bart was not holding a gun on him. That in fact, the waddy's sun-burned hands were lightly resting on the saddle-horn.

'I–' Frank began and licked dry lips with a tongue like sand-paper.

Kroeller grinned wickedly. 'Seems like I ain't ever seen a rustler so goddam' guilty as yuh, Frankie boy. Ain't only showin' in thet carcase over yonder an' the cut-up hide, it's shore enough printed all over yore face, Hervey–'

'Listen Bart–' The boy's voice was little better than the croak of a bull-frog.

'I ain't figgerin' on *listening* to anythin', Frankie boy. I'm kinda content with doin' the talkin' and jest *lookin'*!

'Better drop that toy gun, too, afore I plug yuh!' Kroeller's voice had lost its easy mocking drawl, had roughened noticeably.

'Don't make me do that, Frankie, else I'm gonna miss the pleasure o' seein' yuh kickin' at the end of a rope! Yeah, that's what we do to cattle-thieves, or didn't yuh know thet?'

The natural instinct for self-preservation was belatedly releasing Frank from the thralldom of stark fear.

His brain started to race with lightning speed, even though his body remained still as a statue.

He knew well enough, like everyone else in the valley, the fate of proven rustlers. And, there could be no argument over a man caught in the act with a skinned steer at his feet. It made no difference if the thief were dealt with by rancher or by lawman. The result was the same. A neck-tie party at the nearest tall tree! A one-way ticket, and the light going out for good and always!

Frank thought of the tenuous pattern of

his plans for Saturday and the extent to which his ambitions were already shaping; a partner! weapons! good horses! a sure getaway with money for the taking–'

All these thoughts and feelings swept through him in little more than it took Bart Kroeller to spit, as he sat the pony, pinning the kid with his cold, unforgiving gaze.

Frank had all but finished examining the cards stacked against him. He was sure that Kroeller was alone, otherwise other riders would have shown up by now. And, oddly, the scathing terms the Hatchet man had used, came back to taunt Frank now. Kroeller had called him 'sonny' and 'Frankie boy'. Had despised him for his youth even to the extent of not bothering with his holstered gun!

A bitter anger began to burn away the feeling of sick despair in Frank Hervey's heart. Mebbe he would show this Dillon gunsel something! Make him wish he had shown more respect – but by then it would be too late for Bart Kroeller to indulge in self-recrimination!

The loaded deer rifle was not the weapon Frank would have picked had he the choice. Not for close-quarter shooting. Yet, if he had been wearing the Colt's, it would have been a case of matching speed of draw with this experienced fighter and he could never hope, in his wildest dreams, to beat Bart

Kroeller in a six-gun duel!

But he was already gripping the light but accurate rifle, his fore-finger even through the trigger-guard! Maybe Bart was over confident in facing a kid, albeit an armed one. Maybe he figured a Hervey couldn't do better than knock down a standing steer at close range!

Frank calculated his chances in one last, breathless survey. If they were going to get him, he might as well fight back–

But, impatient now, Bart stirred in the saddle, opening his mouth to speak and simultaneously moving his right hand away from the horn.

He was by no means slow or laggardly, yet Frank had only to elevate the rifle's muzzle by a few inches to obtain what he fervently prayed was the exact angle.

There was no time to throw rifle to shoulder as he had done in dropping the steer. He had to fire from the hip and in less than a second Kroeller would likely explode into killer-action!

The deer rifle's foresight swung up and stayed steady and, too late, Bart saw that his contempt for the kid was a mistake. Even then he was no more than temporarily shaken.

Nearly twenty paces separated them and Kroeller had seen more than one man die as a result of an over-hurried first shot. Besides which, the kid had only pointed the gun. He wouldn't fire—

The rifle cracked as Bart's fingers clawed for the six-gun at his side. A look of shocked incredulity swam into his eyes and slowly vanished, leaving them as vacant of expression as two glass marbles...

Frank was powerless to wrench his gaze from the scene in front of him. This was the first time he had seen a man die; the first time *he* had killed and the dawning realization brought sweat to his face and a sickening nausea in the stomach.

He was still holding the smoking gun at the same uplifted angle, when Kroeller's sagging body slid from the saddle, causing the cow-pony to cavort and suddenly bound away.

Hervey dragged his gaze away as the wagon's team pulled restively at the traces. Quickly transferring the rifle to his left hand, he checked on the tied reins and brake lever, figuring they would suffice unless the team really stampeded.

His quick, searching glance swept over the immediate terrain and then on to the brush and tree-lined sections of the river. As far as he could see, nothing moved except some far-distant cattle and a few birds wheeling high against the blue sky.

Well, Bart's horse had bolted and sooner or later it would make its way home, perhaps stopping to graze on the way. Possibly, Frank figured, he had a couple of hours' grace, maybe more, but he couldn't bank on it!

He went to work on the carcass with a frantic, desperate haste and determination which yet lent him an unusual strength.

Before loading the huge cuts of meat, he brought the wagon as near to the dead beast as he dared, sparing the time to hobble the team as an added precaution.

Whilst he worked, he glanced up periodically, rifle at hand, half-fearing the arrival of other Hatchet riders. Yet nothing occurred to disturb him save when he was forced to grip the rear wagon wheel as a sick giddiness overtook him.

He knew that it was the reaction from killing a man and knew also, that it was something he had to conquer.

He forced himself to walk over and gaze down at the dead Bart Kroeller, remained looking at the man for all of two minutes, remembering he had been a paid killer, remembering also that it had been either Kroeller's life or his own!

He was a trifle unsure of what Hatchet would make of the scene he was about to leave. The ground was scuffed up some and stained here and there with brown splotches. Wheel-tracks were clear where he had driven the wagon over the green, spring grass, but maybe, by the time they found Kroeller, the sign wouldn't be so dam' clear.

In any case, Frank told himself, even though they'll know a steer's been killed an' stolen and a wagon's been here, no one could *prove* anything. Nor would they be able to say who killed Kroeller!

Shortly, he rolled the strips of hide as tightly as he could and stowed them in the wagon. These he would bury someplace on the homestead and make some plausible excuse to Dave if he should ask about the skin.

Once again he cast his glance over the scene, feeling an increasing flow of confidence that neither Dillon nor Wildcat's lawmen could point the finger at him, with no more evidence than lay here.

But, as he was bending down to unhobble the team, his eye caught the glint of lowering sun on metal, a yard or so away.

He reached forward and retrieved the spent cartridge which he must have unthinkingly ejected from the rifle. He regarded it thoughtfully, seeing it for the first time as a piece of damning evidence! Whoever had found this would likely have deduced that Bart had been killed by someone owning a .22 rifle. And, in country where heavier calibre guns were normally used, such a find might well prove fatally conclusive!

There were not many .22 calibre rifles used in Crooked River Valley *and most everyone would know the Herveys owned one!*

With a shudder of relief, Frank walked to the water's edge and hurled the spent cartridge clear into the middle of the smoothly flowing Crooked River.

By the time he had driven back on to Hervey land, the boy was beginning to feel a little easier in both mind and body...

It was still dark when Frank stepped silently from his room, groped his way across to the table and lit the lamp.

His eyes moved swiftly to Ma's ancient and battered wall-clock, the bent hands of which showed a few minutes after 3.30 a.m.

He let go a sigh of relief. Sure of the exact time now, he could afford to prepare without haste for the day which was soon to dawn.

Completely dressed except for boots, he padded to the store-cupboard and filled a bandana with bread, meat, a wedge of pie, afterwards securely tying the kerchief's four corners together.

He paused for a moment, holding the wrapped-up food, and thought back for a moment on the two preceding days.

It seemed an age since Thursday when he had killed Bart Kroeller, had butchered the steer and toted it back home to receive

Dave's and Ma's acclaim for his efforts.

Somehow, he had managed to eat supper without choking and had successfully managed to answer questions and even engage in small talk without exciting suspicion. It had been tough going until Dave, noticing his increasing stiffness of movement, had ordered him to bed, suggesting that Frank should take things easy the following day.

That restful day yesterday, had been a lifesaver, enabling Frank to work the punishing ache from his muscles gradually and giving him a chance to recover somewhat from the shock and horror of Thursday's fateful event...

With a muttered curse, Frank pushed the thoughts from him, anxious as he was to be on his way before either Dave or Ma should wake. Not that there was any secret about his early morning departure, for, in the belief Frank was spending the day in Caprock, Ma had left food in the cupboard overnight and Dave had insisted he took the buckskin again.

If they had been surprised to learn he would be setting out well before dawn, they both put it down to the boy's natural desire to make a day of it and derive the full maximum from the outing.

No, it was just that he didn't feel like Ma's chatter right now, or Dave's well-meaning remarks. Why, the poor fool might even suggest packing Ma off someplace for the day and riding along with him clear to Caprock!

There was no reason for Frank to delay longer and, turning the lamp low, he picked up his brogans and soft-footed out of the house and across the starlit yard to the barns.

By the time he had saddled and bridled the horse, dawn was a suffused glow across the eastern horizon. He had to curb the frisky buckskin, holding it to an enforced walk. It would need all that steam before today was through, Frank thought with grim humour, heading towards the secret cache at the creek's edge. Once there, he ground-tied the pony and quickly lifted the top stones of the cairn, groping for boots, cartridge-belt and gun. Both the latter, together with the ammunition box, he had previously wrapped in pieces of old blanket and oilskin to preserve them from the damp.

It was the work of only a few moments to buckle on the shell-belt and gun and pull on the cowboots, afterwards placing his heavy work shoes into the stone cavity and withdrawing the two large corked jars of stain and the smaller bottles of bleach and spirit solvent.

He used the blanket strips to protect them, before tying bottles and jars securely in the blanket roll at the saddle cantle.

From his crouched down position, he peered through the protecting scrub and brush along the shallow bank, towards the house. Although the living-room window was at an acute angle from this particular viewpoint, he thought that the lamplight glow appeared brighter. Probably Dave was up and fooling around with the stove. It was time to be moving!

He forded the creek and set out, half-confident, half-fearful about the ultimate outcome of his carefully laid plans...

As the sun climbed and touched the snow-topped Magpies with its reaching golden rays, Frank put the buckskin to a cut-bank which would bring him to within a half-mile or so of the hidden arroyo.

Whilst his senses had been keenly alert throughout this vital ride for any possible threat of danger, his mind had probed speculatively into the possible repercussions of Thursday's affair.

So far, no one had come busting over from Hatchet to hurl accusations at the Herveys. Neither had Lack or Fiedler made a routine check-up. That could mean either Bart's body had not yet been found, or else Dillon was deciding to play it close to his vest.

Frank found himself favouring the latter theory, which seemed to bear out his original idea that whatever Hatchet *thought* they couldn't *accuse* the Herveys without tangible evidence acceptable to the law. And, Frank grinned, there was no such evidence!

The slaughtered steer was now nothing more than butcher's meat, hanging in the Hervey's cellar. The hide, with its brand rendered unidentifiable by Frank's knife, lay carefully buried at a spot unlikely to be either found or examined.

Moreover, neither Dave nor Ma had questioned the plausible explanation that he had sold the several strips of hide to a wagoner trailing along Crooked River towards Stella.

Dave had only laughed. 'You did well enough Frank,' he had said. 'Single hides ain't worth much unless they're in one piece and then no more'n six-seven dollars, mebbe...'

All in all, Frank was certain that Lady Luck still rode at his stirrup! And there was no anxious waiting at the arroyo this time.

To his relief, Emma rode in only a few minutes after he had dismounted and tied the buckskin.

He saw at once that she had sheared her long black hair close like a man's. The dark, bony face, the wiry, almost masculine figure, merely added to the general illusion. Even from a few yards' distance, she looked like a young, hard-faced cow puncher.

He nodded approvingly and handed her

some of the bread and meat which he had brought. They ate quickly and drank canteen water to quench their immediate thirsts.

Before setting to work on the roans, Frank made sure they were securely tied. Emma shed the calf-skin vest, evidently prepared to do her share of work under Hervey's direction.

Soon, in spite of protests from the horses themselves, the roan geldings began to acquire an astonishingly different appearance.

Frank was worried because the two large jars of stain might be insufficient for the job. But they managed to eke it out, spreading it on thinly with cloths, clear down to the animals' white stockings.

The stuff dried quickly and, a couple of hours after starting, Hervey and Emma stood back to admire their handiwork.

'Mebbe they wouldn't stand up to a right careful inspection,' he grinned, 'but—'

'Ain't nobody gonna go over 'em with a enlargin' glass,' Emma grunted, secretly amazed at the successful disguise.

Frank nodded. 'If you wanta go blonde, there's bleach in this bottle,' he told her. 'Ain't much use me usin' it 'less I dye it back again before tonight!'

Some while later, two range-rigged men riding black geldings and leading a buckskin cow-pony, headed for the outskirts of Caprock along a series of brush-choked cut-offs.

A half-mile outside town, Hervey un-shipped and transferred himself to the buckskin's saddle. Oddly enough, even in the excitement of what lay ahead, he did not fail to remember about the clock he was going to get for Ma, nor the twenty-five dollars in his pants' pocket, which Dave had advanced him for that very purpose.

Emma knew there was scarcely a chance anyone would ride along this narrow trail to nowhere, and spot her in the cottonwood grove, holding two black horses. But for once in her life she was as nervous and jumpy as a cat. Time dragged on intermin-ably as she smoked one quirly after another. Could Frank have been delayed by someone in Caprock? *Had he already done something for which the law might be after him!*

When at last she spotted him heading towards the trees, walking alone and confident, she let go her pent-up breath in a snake-like hiss of angry relief...

CHAPTER 8

THE RAID!

Most of Wildcat's inhabitants were still indoors, either finishing a late noon meal or idling away a half-hour before going about their business. A few oldsters lounged back in tilted chairs under shady porches, sleepily watching the slow ripples of life on Main. An occasional rider walked his horse to the rack fronting the Lucky Strike; several traders talked business either amongst themselves or with the few chance customers.

Sheriff Lack waddled ponderously from his cottage to his office, mopping his forehead with a dirty handkerchief and scratching his pot-belly a couple of times.

Pearl Gallina emerged from the saloon, moved with a seductively swaying gait towards Gertrude Melias's dress-making establishment.

Wey Blessiter, fat, florid and full of his own self-importance, stepped from the bank and clambered into the waiting carriage, issuing one terse word of command to the liveried black on the driving-seat. The

115

carriage rolled smoothly towards the white-painted Blessiter residence on the Hill.

Will Fiedler leaned against the door jamb, spreading his gaze over the street's peaceful, gentle activity. By craning his neck he had just about been able to watch Blessiter step into the carriage, without the necessity of moving his body from where it propped up the sheriff's doorway. He fired a half-smoked stogie and cursed quietly as Lack's voice boomed at him from back of the office.

And, as the deputy turned inside, two dust-powdered riders walked their horses slowly up East Street and pulled in at the junction of Main.

Probably, if Lack had not summoned his deputy at that precise moment, Fiedler would have glimpsed the two strangers and amused himself by some idle speculation as to their identity, employment, purpose in town, ultimate destination, and the like!

By such slim threads of chance hang the fortunes and very lives of many a man or woman...

With casual unconcern, the taller of the two riders slid from leather and moved easily, but with far-reaching strides across the boardwalk.

Even if Fiedler, or some such interested citizen, had been able to observe the man closely, it was doubtful he would have been identified as young Hervey without a

116

second or third penetrating glance.

He wore a very ordinary stetson, alkali dust rendering its colour vague and difficult of description; a plain, dark woollen shirt; waist overalls and worn down half-boots. Like any of Dillon's riders, he toted a holstered gun on a filled shell-belt.

His face, what could be seen of it under the hat-brim shadow, was dark and blackly stubbled as though he was starting a full beard. The usual range-rider's bandana was knotted around his neck, as indeterminate in appearance and colour as the rest of his dust-stippled garb.

His hands were empty except for what appeared to be a tightly folded piece of sackcloth, perhaps even a flour- or wheat-sack.

But no one in town at that exact moment was near enough by a hundred yards to observe these finer details. Even the idling oldsters scattered in tip-tilted chairs were only half aware that a couple of hands from someplace had ridden into town, maybe for their boss.

But, with the closing of the glass-panelled doors behind him, a swift change came over Frank Hervey's lazily deliberate movements.

In a flash, his head dipped down, left hand raising the neckerchief from chin to nose bridge, right hand whipping the Colt's gun from leather and cocking the hammer in a single fluid action.

So swiftly and quietly had he engineered his entry and switched from the role of casual citizen to that of a masked bandit, so slick and smooth was the transformation, that neither Simon Churt nor the solitary customer, engrossed as they were, had even glanced his way.

It was the kid's sharp-sounding action of sliding home the door bolts and drawing down the blinds which caused Churt to look up quickly and immediately turn a sickly pallor as he stared unbelievingly at the sinister, masked figure, half crouched there with naked gun pointed unwaveringly at the teller's chest.

'*Git yore hands up, both o' you!*' Frank swung the Colt's barrel a fraction to include the man who he now identified as Max Cassen, owner of the Lucky Strike.

Churt's hands went up quickly. Cassen was a mite slow until Frank strode forward and jabbed him in the belly with the gun barrel, prodding him back against the wall, face turned inwards. Fortunate indeed for Cassen that the cocked hammer did not fall as a result of that quick, rough action.

Like quicksilver, Frank darted across to the safe, signalled the teller with his gun.

'*Open it – fast!*'

'I–' Churt began, and moved a dry tongue over trembling lips.

'You got jest ten seconds,' the voice behind

the dark mask rasped. 'I'm gonna start countin' – *now!*'

But Simon Churt needed no second bidding. He figured he knew a bluff when he saw one, and *this* man was not bluffing.

With unsteady hands, the teller inserted a key. Evidently the combination was set at neutral for the heavy door swung open to his touch, revealing bundles of notes neatly tied, and leathern pokes bulging with coin.

Swiftly the masked man swept bills and gold pokes into the sack he held, keeping one eye on the two uneasily restless men. His sweeping gaze took in smaller quantities of money neatly stacked behind the counter grille. These he swept into the sack with the gun barrel.

Cassen, unarmed, looked around wildly for some improvised weapon, or for some means of giving an alarm. But, swift as a striking rattler, the bandit's gun crashed down on to his head. Cassen's eyes glazed, his body slackened and slumped to the floor.

Simon Churt's eyes dilated with fear. His mouth opened wide but the desperate cry was never uttered for again the gun rose and descended with relentless force and purpose. Churt's arms had gone up in an instinctive gesture of self-preservation, but he failed completely to ward off the sickening blow which knocked him across the counter where he lay for a few seconds before sliding lower and lower until ending in a crumpled heap against the counter base.

The sweat was running from Hervey's hat brim, trickling into his eyes. He tugged the bandana down and hastily wiped face and neck with a shaking arm.

The clock on the wall showed four minutes after two o'clock and Hervey wondered how such an eternity of desperate action could be packed into so short a period of time. Four minutes only – nearly five, since he had dismounted outside, and in his left hand was a tightly held sack stuffed with wealth, and straight ahead lay the way to freedom!

He reholstered the gun and his spirits began to soar with the realization that luck still tagged him. No one had hammered on the bolted doors, demanding admittance, an event which might well have spelled disaster to the raid.

One quick, backward glance at the two unconscious men and the kid was at the doors, releasing the bolts and raising the blinds.

The street appeared to be about the same as when he had entered, except that the rear wheels of a vehicle were just visible at the boardwalk's edge.

Mebbe it's Cassen's rig, Frank thought,

opening the door, and then remembered that there had been no vehicle outside, five minutes ago!

His head was again slightly downbent, his movements, despite every appearance to the contrary, deceptively fast. So much so, he was unable to avoid collision with another figure, hurrying towards the bank doors.

It was not so much that they met with any solid impact, as that the sudden un-expectedness of it, momentarily threw both of them off-balance.

Frank swore under his breath as he lurched sideways, his narrowed, venomous glance going out to the red-haired girl who had half fallen against a roof-post.

Surprise and pain lay in her smouldering green eyes, changing swiftly to bright anger as she read the man's expression, watched him in astonishment as he turned away and half ran the few yards to the street corner.

Sorrel Sperry saw the rumps and swishing tails of two black horses. She saw the man slip round the bank's corner and noticed in retrospect as it were, that he carried a bulging sack in his left hand.

There was something extraordinarily strange about the whole set-up she thought, hearing now the jingle of bit chains and the soft clip-clop of hooves in the dust.

When she looked again, the horses' rumps were no longer visible and, on a sudden

121

hunch, Sorrel moved quickly to the corner and laid her gaze down East Street through the stirring dust.

They had travelled about a quarter-mile, not racing, but neither loitering. The other rider appeared to be of very slight build, Sorrel thought, though it was impossible to observe any salient details at this distance and with the yellow dust eddying over the street.

She turned back, promising herself to give that dark, unshaven young man a piece of her mind if or when she should set eyes on him again.

But there was still something disturbing the surface of her being, quite apart from the first surge of anger at such loutish manners.

It was, Sorrel thought suddenly, *almost as though he had something to hide!* That sack, for instance, what might it have contained? Certainly not flour or wheat by its very shape, and the ease with which the man had gripped it, one handedly.

Sorrel Sperry knew well enough about the bulk and weight of a bushel sack filled with grain. Even allowing for a man's superior strength–

She broke off the train of thought, and of a sudden, ran to the bank entrance pushing at the nearest swing door and bursting into the room with a violence that sent papers kiting into the air before descending in slow

122

spirals to the floor.

It took Sorrel's eyes but a few seconds to adapt themselves to the duller light in here and then she saw Max Cassen's bulky figure sprawled against one wall. A thin rivulet of blood had trickled from his head to his left ear. He was breathing noisily and Sorrel Sperry knew a quick relief that the man was alive.

She stepped towards the counter, only then seeing Churt's huddled figure, face waxy as candle-grease. The safe door stood open, enabling her to view the empty interior.

She stood quite still, absorbing the full significance of the scene, before swinging round sharply and running out on to the boardwalk.

Sorrel's urgent glance flashed from left to right, embracing a trio of traders, a few men and women walking slowly along the opposite walk, six-seven oldsters, dozing in front of the barber shop, a lone cowboy emerging unsteadily from the Lucky Strike, a few kids playing–There seemed to be nobody near enough for quick action and quite unhysterically, Sorrel Sperry opened her mouth wide and emitted the most piercing and blood-curdling scream that ever Wildcat had heard since the last Indian scare.

Faces immediately appeared at windows, figures launched themselves through doorways with such jack-in-the-box-like force that at any other time, the scene might have appeared ludicrous to the point of farcical comedy. But Sorrel's lips were now firmly compressed, her eyes bright with shocked anger. Mentally, she was picturing the wounded Max Cassen as she had seen him only a few moments before; and the other man, probably the teller, who had lain there so still and deathly white.

The street which had dozed in the early afternoon, had now found itself rudely awakened.

Men in shirt-sleeves and under-vests, some clutching shotguns, and women still apron-decked, surged forward to where the girl stood beckoning.

The portly figure of Sheriff Lack spilled out from the crowd, followed a moment later by the thin shape of Will Fiedler.

'The bank's bin robbed, Sheriff!' Sorrel called and whirled towards the doors, Lack hurrying breathlessly on her heels.

Fiedler gained the plankwalk before any of those in the surging throng.

He buttonholed Dick Maury and pinned his own deputy's badge on to the gunsmith's shirt.

'Stick right here, Dick, an' don't let nobody through...'

By the time they had reached the point where East Street faded and merged into scrub- and brush-stippled ridges, Frank Hervey had stopped shaking.

During the actual raid, tense though he had been, brain and muscles had co-ordinated to a hair-trigger degree.

But reaction, combined with the shock of that split-second collision with the un-known girl, had left him groggy at the knees. Twice in mounting, his boot had slipped from the oxbow stirrup and only when Emma had grabbed the sack and extended a muscular helping hand, had Frank hit leather with a bone-shaking jolt.

He turned in the saddle for the third or fourth time, seeing nothing but an empty street behind them. For the first time he grinned, touching the girl's arm excitedly.

'We made it, Emma! We got the edge on 'em now, whenever they like to start! See thet cottonwood stand? Well, beyond is where we turn down into the creek bed. C'm on now! Let's do some ridin'!'

She flashed him a smile, handed the filled sack across and bent to the task of keeping level despite sharp twists and turns and sudden bursts of speed.

They clattered along the dried up water-course, compelled to ride more carefully over the rock-strewn bed. Twice Frank motioned to pull up, both of them listening for any sounds of pursuit.

'Mebbe they don't even savvy which way

we's ridin'! Mebbe they don't know there's *bin* a raid–'

'They know all right,' Frank told her and added coolly, 'an' they'll be ridin' after us soon. Lack ain't much use, but Fiedler'll git a posse together, an' the girl will sure tell 'em we headed down East Street!'

Rapidly he gave her a brief outline of what had taken place, confining himself to bare essentials and pausing every so often to look around and listen.

Emma's eyes narrowed down to slits. She didn't like that news about the dame! Her glance moved over to the wheatsack now secured across Hervey's saddle.

'How much yuh figger–?'

Frank shook his head impatiently. 'Didn't stop to count it!' His tone was heavy with sarcasm and she shut her mouth like a steel trap, spurring her mount as Hervey put his horse to the first of the lateral grassy ridges, west of Wildcat.

Before descending, he swung his gaze round, carefully surveyed their back-trail. Nothing moved along the curving river bed. No vision of angry possemen met Frank's smiling eyes. No sounds of pursuit abraded the now smooth surface of his mind.

Why, it was sure enough possible, mebbe likely, that Fiedler would lose their sign at the cottonwoods. There was nothing for a white man to pick up along the rock- and boulder-strewn bed...

Despite the absence of pursuit so far, the kid insisted on sticking to his original plan; to ride clear through Lobo Cañon and circle back rather than arrow straight for the hideout.

At somewhere around three-thirty o'clock, they descended the arroyo, mounts sweating and dusty, the riders themselves stiff from long hours in the saddle.

Emma watered the horses, half from each canteen poured into her stetson, whilst Frank began counting the money.

She joined him presently, eyes avidly watching the growing stacks of bills and coins. It seemed an interminable period before Frank raised a shining face and announced a haul of three thousand, five hundred and ten dollars!

'So it paid off like yuh said, Frank!'

He nodded. 'Better'n I ever expected. This'll keep us goin' fer awhile–'

'What about the *next* one? Yuh got somethin' lined up mebbe?'

'We're gonna wait 'till the shindig over *this* job cools down first,' he growled, apportioning bills and gold pieces into two equal stacks.

'Don't make the mistake o' thinkin' Wildcat's gonna take this lyin' down. They's gonna be some action before long, or I miss my guess!...'

Well before dusk, he was moving around Caprock, making himself seen in various saloons and stores.

After leading the buckskin to the livery where it was well-fed and watered, he purchased the Swiss clock, a checkered shirt and a red silk bandana.

He had to be careful how he walked for every available pocket was stuffed with bills or twenty-dollar pieces! Across the street, Marshal Cal Hockin sauntered along the plankwalk nodding now and again to passers-by. Frank had seen Caprock's law man on several occasions before and now he crossed the street to a restaurant, casually acknowledging the marshal before going inside.

With a substantial meal under his belt, he rode the J.H. buckskin out of town, experiencing an elation he had never before known. Everything had gone off, smooth as silk; exactly as planned.

He had ridden off before dawn this morning, a ragged, penniless sod-buster, forced to rely on the generosity or otherwise of brother Dave. Now, through careful planning and some astounding good luck, he was worth seventeen hundred and fifty bucks!

The hell of it was, most of it would have to remain stashed away some place until such time as he could make a clean break from the family and take up a new life and a new name, some place else.

But he was not blind to the great advantage that was his, in being able to use the family and the homestead as a cover for further raids. Uneasily now, he began worrying over Simon Churt. He hadn't meant to hit the old man quite so hard and Churt had sure looked bad lying there in a crumpled heap on the floor!

Frank shuddered as the scene formed clearly in his mind's eye, presenting him with an all too clear picture of both teller and saloon keeper inert and unconscious on the bank's floor.

Not that he was over anxious about Max Cassen. It would take more than a heavy gun-butt to floor Cassen for any length of time!

But Churt, now, he was a mite different. Some of these oldsters were dam' brittle; cracked more easily than a man would expect.

The sudden thought that he might have killed *two* men within the space of three days, brought Frank out in another cold sweat.

Only by forcing his thoughts into other channels – an ability which he was rapidly beginning to develop – was he finally able to relax in the saddle and put the buckskin to a steady, mile-consuming lope...

CHAPTER 9

DILLON'S PRICE

Dillon's hard gaze moved over the scene, registering the slightly scuffed grass, the few almost invisible brown stains, the faint wheel-tracks–

Gucht stood by his ground-tied pony, knotted fists digging into his waist, angry glance swivelling back to the Hatchet owner's face. Three Hatchet riders sat their mounts a few yards back.

'Well, the sign's clear enough to me, Walt,' Gucht snarled. 'Reckon it is to Butch, an' Hodo an' Smith, likewise!

'This is Dave Hervey's dirty work! Them Herveys has allus hated us, Walt, but mebbe you cain't see it on account of Clovis–'

'Clovis Hervey don't come into it, Munro. If I was to marry her tomorrow, it shore wouldn't stop me settlin' with Dave or Frank, was we sure one of 'em was responsible fer killin' Bart an' butcherin' a steer. Besides which–'

'You can rule Frank out,' Gucht snapped. 'He ain't dry behind the ears yet, an' another thing, it was Dave jumped me at

Sperry's on account he's hot for that woman. Ain't never seen a man so all-fired jealous– Hell! never mind that. The point is, them wheel tracks are pointin' near enough south-east, straight for Spanish Creek. If you don't want to bring the law in on this, surely to God we can settle it our *own* way, Walt?'

'Leave me to do the decidin', Mun,' Dillon grated. 'Sure *we* know you hate Dave's guts, but that don't prove anythin'.

'I kin read the sign as well, but since Hatchet made its own law in the valley, we got a sheriff with county powers, remember? Ride over an' blast Dave Hervey an' even Herb Lack'd have to stir himself even if it meant gettin' a U.S. Marshal from Stella.'

'Yuh figger to let Hervey get away with murderin' Bart?' Butch Corrigan asked coldly.

'We'll find out fer sure who did it. Mebbe it was Dave, mebbe someone else. When we do, we either hand 'em over to Lack, if we got enough proof to make the charge stick, else we string 'em up ourselves an' *claim* they was caught red-handed!'

Gucht relaxed a little. 'I've got a score to settle, Walt–'

'Sure you have an' you kin square it any time you figger to beat Dave. But I'm warnin' you-all, *don't* draw on a man as ain't totin' a gun and *don't* use his back fer a target. Because sure as hell, Lack an' Fiedler'd have enough to haul you up on a murder charge!'

Gucht almost said, *I drew on the so-and-so at Sperry's and he wasn't totin' a gun!*

'The day Hatchet ain't big enough to handle its own enemies, I quit,' Butch Corrigan growled.

'Then you won't ever quit,' Dillon snapped. 'But any o' you go off half-cocked like you was suggestin', you won't *need* to quit. They'll *haul* you away!

'Now let's take Bart along an' bury him. I'm figurin' on ridin' over to Spanish Creek come Saturday. Mebbe I kin find out a few things.'

But, the idea that Dillon had in mind was not quite the same one as he had given his foreman and the Hatchet riders to understand. He smiled as he rode behind the others, thinking how nice it would be to have Clovis Hervey up at the house permanently as his wife!

The chore of punishing Bart's killer, whether it were Dave or Frank or anyone else, could be dealt with later...

There was no sign of either of the boys, this Saturday morning as Dillon crossed the creek and entered the yard, which was just exactly the way Walt wanted it.

He climbed down, tied the gelding's reins as Ma appeared at the open door.

Reluctantly, she bade him 'light down for coffee'. A tardy invitation, as Walt was already tromping his way to the door.

Setting his face into a sober expression and his big frame into a chair, Walt lifted his gaze to the woman's face as she poured two cups of coffee.

'Where's the boys, Clovis?'

She replaced the pot on top of the stove and seated herself across the table from Dillon.

'Frank's having himself a day in Caprock. Ain't had much time off lately. Dave's out startin' on brandin'. Why do you ask?'

Walt stirred his coffee and drank noisily.

'I'm glad they're not around for the moment, Clovis. You see,' he continued, leaning forward and gazing searchingly at Ma's face, 'mebbe I got some bad news fer you. I don't rightly know yet–'

'Bad news?' Ma's heart fluttered in her breast. What was Walt driving at? What was he looking so deadly serious about?

'You ain't gotta say anythin' about this, Clovis, not to *anyone*, least of all Dave or Frank, but we's pretty certain at Hatchet that – Frank, mebbe Dave, but *we* figger it was Frank, butchered a steer yesterday–'

'*Oh!*' Ma's hand flew to her mouth. Her eyes were wide open as she stared back at Dillon.

'Mebbe even 'twas Thursday,' Walt

133

amended. 'But we's sure missin' a big beef crittur an' the sign's there to read, Clovis! Bloodstains on the grass, ground kinda scuffed up an' wagon tracks—'

'*Wagon* tracks!' Ma held her breath for a moment. Frank had ridden out on Thursday afternoon to slaughter and skin a mossy-horn and at dusk, he had returned *in the wagon,* with the steer butchered and cut-up! He had seemed more shaken than need be on his return. Had scarcely eaten his supper. Ma had put it down to the boy's inexperience, thinking the bloody work might have upset him. But why should it? she asked herself now. He had been along with Dave many times before and had never reacted like that at the sight of a skinned carcase!

'You seem to recall somethin', Clovis,' Walt said softly.

Ma chastened herself for having so little control over her features. She managed a smile now, deliberately making herself provocative, lowering dark lashes on to her cheeks, moistening her lips so that they pouted wetly and revealed her white teeth in a teasing smile.

'If Frank killed one of *your* steers, Walt,' she said in a voice as thick as molasses, 'I'll not only beat the living daylights outa him, growed up though he is, I'll make him bring over a "J.H." steer an' he can watch you overbrand it with a Hatchet, Walt! How does that suit you?'

'Fine, Clovis. Jest fine.' His voice was husky, but he schooled himself to keep his thoughts running the way he had planned.

On a sudden inspiration, Dillon had decided not to nominate Dave as the candidate for stealing but *Frank,* shrewdly realizing as he did that whatever Dave's virtues were, or whatever Frank's short-comings, it was the younger son who could best be used as a threat! Often enough the Hatchet owner had intercepted a mother's glance of yearning, directed, not towards the self-sufficient and capable Dave, but towards the weaker, less responsible son!

Dillon had unreservedly agreed with Gucht that Frank Hervey could be ruled out as the rustler-killer, and, only on the ride over to Spanish Creek had he conceived the idea which, amazingly now, appeared to be paying dividends!

Frank *had* driven out in a wagon on Thursday, and the kid *had* killed a steer, probably make out to Ma and Dave it was one of their own! Was this whole thing too much of a coincidence or did young Hervey possess hidden depths, a hitherto un-revealed toughness and gun-prowess?

Suddenly, Dillon found himself on safer ground. There *couldn't* be any doubt now! Frank Hervey had not only rustled a

Hatchet steer, but, interrupted by Bart, *the kid had killed one of Hatchet's fastest gunfighters!*

'But that ain't all, Clovis,' Walt purred. 'If it was jest a question of pullin' down one steer, well–' He shrugged expansively.

'What d'you mean, Walt – "that ain't all"?'

'Reckon mebbe Frank meant no harm. I guess it was jest his idea of a joke to kill one of my steers. But Bart Kroeller horned in, an' whoever shot thet steer, *shot Bart clear through the heart!*'

Ma's face drained itself of colour. The coquette in her, through which she had hoped to divert Walt's attention from Frank to herself, vanished like smoke on a wind.

Twice she tried to speak, but each time the words stuck in her mouth, Dillon, softening, drew a flask from his pocket and sloshed liquor into both coffee cups.

'Drink it, Clovis!'

He had to repeat the command in a harsher voice before she put the cup to her lips, even then only reacting with the mechanical precision of a machine. But when she returned cup to saucer, they rattled together with a violence that betrayed the trembling panic sweeping over her.

'You – you must be – wrong, Walt! There's some kinda mistake! Frank ain't – he ain't a killer. Surely you know that, Walt? *Walt! Tell me there's bin a mistake made–*'

136

'There cain't be any mistake, honey,' Dillon murmured, soothingly. 'You know as well as I do, Frank pulled down a Hatchet steer an' I'm tellin' you, Clovis, the same hombre as brought you in a wagon-load o' meat last Thursday, shot Bart stone dead! The sign's clear enough to read. Why, I had a job to stop Munro an' a bunch of the boys ridin' over, there an' then to – well, I guess in the mood they was in, more killin' would 'a' been done–'

'You – you mean Gucht was set to ride over here *and gun down, Frank?*' Stark horror showed in Ma's face, rendering her lovely eyes muddy, her expressive mouth tight-drawn to an ugly line.

He nodded, reaching forward and laying a calloused hand on her bare fore-arm. 'You got me to thank that they didn't. They wasn't particular whether it was Frank or Dave. Either one would 'a' done. You gotta try an' see it their way, honey. Sure, they's rough men mebbe, but loyal to Hatchet. Stock stealin's a hangin' offence even if we do joke about it now an' agin. Moreover, one o' their saddle-pards was murdered! How d'you think they feel?'

'You *can't* say it was – murder, Walt! Mebbe Bart Kroeller drew first! Mebbe Frank jest *had* to shoot to save his own life! It was self-defence, Walt,' she cried wildly. 'It *musta* bin self-defence. Frank wouldn't–'

137

She broke off suddenly, staring wide-eyed at Dillon. The Hatchet owner was shaking his big head slowly and sorrowfully.

'That's what *anybody'd* figger, Clovis, knowin' Frank ain't a bad kid. But there ain't a chance o' puttin' in a plea of self-defence. Y'see, Bart's gun was in its holster, an' it hadn't bin fired–'

'*Plea?*' Ma's grief-stricken gaze moved over the big man's face until Walt was forced to drop his gaze.

'What do you mean by "plea" of self-defence? You ain't figurin'–?'

'Supposin' Munro or Butch or anyone fer that matter, stole a Hervey crittur an' then shot Dave or Frank! You'd want the killer brought in, wouldn't you? What's more, if I know you, Clovis, an' I shore reckon I do, you'd be there, pullin' on the end o' the rope an' yellin' for blood!'

She shivered, sick at Walt's crude assessment of her character; sick with dread at the prospect of her boy being arrested by the sheriff and hauled to Stella, indicted for murder. With so much evidence against him, the verdict would be a foregone conclusion. She could visualize the cruel-faced Gucht giving his damning evidence ably backed by the man Walt had mentioned, Butch Corrigan, and perhaps, to a lesser degree, by Walt himself!

During those moments of Dillon's terrible

revelation, shock and grief and then a clawing fear, held her rigid. Yet, Clovis Hervey had always been possessed of a fierce and irresistible determination, once she had decided that her course was right. But, here she paused, unable to blind herself to the fact that guilt was guilt. There was no gainsaying that the guilty must be punished, not only for the crime but as an example to others!

Oh, God! How simple it all sounded when only others were involved. But what primitive instincts and emotions were bared when one's own beloved ones fell foul both of God's laws and those of the Territory!

Something of this purposeful and rebellious streak began to surge in her now. Perhaps Frank, in some way, had inherited it. He was part of her, like Dave. Why should it not be so?

Rebellious, stubborn, he had gone wild for the moment, flouting law and order, revelling in the act which had, though wrongly, gained them meat enough for months, at Hatchet's expense!

And then, Kroeller had shown up! A man with an evil and dangerous reputation. Frank might well have panicked, swung up the deer rifle and fired blindly; an instinctive action, executed almost in desperate despair. So much could Clovis feel, so much could she understand the boy's behaviour, that the finer concepts of right and wrong melted before the consuming heat of her love.

With the resolve to fight, as a she-cat for its cubs, Clovis Hervey's whole personality seemed to undergo a total transformation. Whereas a short while ago she had played up to Walt with no more than passing coquetry, she now caressed him with her warm, smiling glance.

'If, Walt,' she murmured, 'I promised you thet in a few weeks, say—'

Eagerly he grabbed her arm, the desire for possessing something hitherto denied, firing his blood.

'You mean that, Clovis? You ain't stringin' me along—?'

She shook her head slowly, still smiling, a shaft of sunlight from the window creating around her head a nimbus of gold.

'I ain't stringin' you along, Walt. I mean it, jest so long as you say and do *nothin'* about Frank!

'One word, to Herb or Will or *anyone,* an' so help me God' – she drew a deep breath– 'I'll kill you my own self!'

Dillon shoved back his chair, reached round the table and pulled Clovis Hervey to her feet, crushing her into his arms, eyes alight with triumph.

'I give you my solemn word, honey. You fix the date within four weeks an' if Frank ever meets trouble through me—' He broke off and laughed boisterously. 'You shore have permission to plug me full o' holes!'

She lifted her mouth and kissed him. *Frank is safe!* was the thought that hammered through her brain with fierce exultation!

Ma Hervey had paid a high price but she was content to do so...

No one could possibly have dreamed that Ma Hervey was anything but a wonderfully happy mother with two fine sons. Perhaps, in a strange way, she was in fact happier this Sunday than she had been for many a long month, the moral aspects of Frank's deed having become obscured almost from the beginning by the overwhelming relief at Walt Dillon's promise.

Dave's lamp stood on the polished chest, shining and gleaming with a brightness scarcely stronger than the light in Ma's eyes.

Over the stone hearth, the Swiss clock ticked away merrily and on the table stood the remains of enough food for a couple more birthday celebrations. Iced layer-cake complete with – on Ma's laughing insistence – forty-three candles; flapjacks with butter and molasses; huge plates of sandwiches, containing every available kind of filling; beef, ham, French fried potatoes, onions, spinach, beans, pineapples, cream – everything, Ma thought, with a queer lump in her throat, *except Jo!*

Dillon sat opposite, well fed, prosperous, broadly smiling in between exploring his teeth with a wood pick. Dave, too, was feeling happy, because he felt sure Ma was, and even Frank appeared relaxed and comfortably at ease.

Next to Ma's plate stood an open box in which glittered a diamond necklace and pendant ear-drops to match. For a moment, misgivings clouded her mind as her gaze intercepted the darts of light radiating from the glittering stones.

'That ain't nothin' honey,' Dillon grinned. 'All I could get from Oliver's at short notice. Best that was in the store, o' course. But wait'll I take you to Stella, git you all rigged out in a new outfit, an' – say, come to think of it, Frank's lookin' right smart today! How come, Frank? You ain't found a gold mine or somethin'?'

The boy laughed easily. His confidence had been mounting rapidly all day.

'Fact of the matter is, Walt, like I told Dave, I met up with some hombre I'd grub-staked fer a few bucks, 'bout a coupla years back.

'You kin figger my surprise–' He broke off as Dave pushed his chair back and moved to the door.

'Thought I heard somethin'. Looks like

Herb an' Will. Mebbe,' he smiled, 'they heard about your party, Ma!'

He was still looking out across the creek and missed the by-play going on behind him.

Frank's confident smile had slipped badly. Ma shot him a swift, apprehensive glance and quickly transferred her hardening gaze to Walt's face. Her eyes seemed to hold a cold implacable threat, but Dillon could only shake his head almost imperceptibly, his expression one of genuine innocence.

I don't reckon he would be fool enough to break his word, Ma thought, *but if he has—*

Dave went out to greet the lawmen as they unshipped stiffly and tied their mounts. Inside the house, Walt and Ma and Frank sweated it out in a thick silence, each for a different reason. But, they listened hard enough, and judging from the small talk which carried into the room, Wildcat's officers sounded neighbourly enough.

Lack mopped his red face as he entered, nodding pleasantly to Ma and the two men. But there was a worried expression in the sheriff's pale eyes. Fiedler, as usual, wore a poker face.

Ma struggled with words of welcome, but luckily Dave broke in.

'Rest yourselves an' eat,' he invited them, 'an don't try kiddin' us you didn't know it was Ma's birthday today!'

143

Fiedler allowed himself a tight smile, shook his head.

'Honest we didn't know, Dave.' He turned to Clovis and inclined his head. 'Many happy returns, Ma. You shore don't look as old as them candles says! Reckon yuh got about ten too many there!'

Ma's smile was sweet and controlled. The flush on her cheeks could have been nothing more than the sign of a woman's pleasure at receiving a nice compliment.

Frank thought, *the so-an'-so's sure got sharp eyes! How much do they know, if anythin'?*

Herb Lack reached for a sandwich, stuffed it into his mouth, his bulk overflowing the creaking chair.

He shook his head and as an afterthought removed the dust-powdered stetson.

'Mebbe we'd 'a' looked in earlier, Ma, if we'd 'a' known. But we been a mite busy tryin' to trace a coupla bank robbers! Yeah! Blessiter's was busted into yesterday, around two o'clock an' nigh on cleaned out—'

'*What?*' Dillon's voice was a bull-like roar. He had money in Wey's bank, only a few hundred dollars; chicken-feed certainly, but a wealthy man likes losing money even less than a poor one.

'Who did it, Herb?' Frank could scarcely recognize his own voice. In spite of fast-beating pulses, his tone was level, echoing only a cool interest.

CHAPTER 10

SORREL'S STORY

Lack swallowed and scowled.

He helped himself to another sandwich as Ma rose from her chair.

'Set down, for heaven's sake, Will, an' eat,' she exploded, turning swiftly to the coffee-pot on the stove.

Mildly surprised, Fiedler sat and began following Herb's example and Ma Hervey's advice.

'Who did it, Herb?' Dave repeated Frank's question impatiently.

'We dunno yet,' Lack admitted, 'but we's hopin' to find out before long. Seems a coupla hombres ridin' black hosses pulled up at East and Main. One of 'em lights down an' goes into the bank. Ain't anyone around on the walk close enough to identify him though.

'Inside he throws a gun on Churt an' Max Cassen, shoves Max against the wall an' threatens to blow Churt apart if–'

'But they didn't shoot – kill anyone?' Frank asked boldly. 'I mean, how d'you *know* it all happened like you say?'

145

Lack appeared hurt. 'Even if the bandit *had* killed 'em, I reckon me an' Will could 'a' figgered the thing out. As it was, the jasper – after Churt had opened the safe – knocked 'em both cold, likely with the butt of his gun–'

'Well, how about Churt and Max,' Dave demanded. 'They okay?'

The sheriff nodded. 'Max got a head like a stone, but Churt wasn't so good fer a while. Hadta have six-seven stitches an' it left him purty shaky. But Doc Curry figgers he'll be all right in a coupla days–'

'Thank goodness no one was hurt real bad,' Ma breathed, pouring coffee for the lawmen.

'Yeah! But they got away with around three thousand, six hun'ed dollars. Leastways, thet's as near as Blessiter figgered after we told him–'

'But surely *someone* saw them?' Dave persisted, continuing to ask exactly the questions for which Frank needed an answer. 'We all know Wildcat don't start livenin' up 'till around dark,' he smiled, 'but–'

'Sure! Someone *did* seem 'em,' Fiedler said softly, 'an' we got a swell description!'

'Nobody we know, I guess?' Dave said, unaware of Fiedler's sarcasm.

'Like hell we got a good description!' Lack snorted. 'Don't take no notice o' Will, he shore has a queer sense o' humour.

146

'Yeah! We got a witness, Sorrel Sperry! Aaron's niece or stepdaughter or some-such. *She* saw the one as did the stealin', *close-up an' without any mask on,* an' all she could say was he looked kinda like a young cow-puncher in need of a shave!'

Lack thumped the table with a ham-like fist.

'How in Hades we lawmen expected to make arrests an' stop crime when the public cain't co-operate–'

'Sorrel Sperry struck me as bein' all wool an' a yard wide,' Dave snapped, irritated by Lack's bombastic attitude. 'Seems kinda reasonable to me she only got mebbe a quick glance an' I guess he looked like any other hombre. I mean,' Dave continued as the others listened intently, 'he was not wearin' a mask from what you said and likely enough his gun was tucked away. What reason would Sorrel Sperry or *anyone* have to figger some wanderin' cowpoke as a bank robber!

'Another thing, Herb; the girl only hit Crooked River last week-end. Reckon she wouldn't know who was townsfolk, an' who was strangers ridin' in?'

'You got a point there,' Lack conceded, feeling slightly more amenable to reason.

'Anyways, we got *somethin'* to go on. Miss Sperry saw 'em ride away down East an' claims the other hombre was small an' thin as a rail. No,' the sheriff said, 'she didn't see his face. By the time she'd thought about it, an' got to the bank corner, they was ridin' at a trot, some way along an' sendin' up a dust curtain.'

'Anything we can do to help, Herb?' Dave said straddling a chair and building a smoke. 'How's about tracks; reckon it ain't likely you picked up any?'

Lack smiled for the first time and nodded to his deputy. 'Ask Will,' he wheezed.

'Sure,' Fiedler drawled. 'We cut some sign after runnin' around in circles all Saturday afternoon. 'Twas faint enough an' we sure ended up with a big question mark 'bout a mile from Lobo Cañon.'

'All you know fer sure then,' Frank said, 'is they lit outa town an' headed west?'

'That's right, Frank.'

'We also know they was ridin' big blacks with white stockin's,' Lack grunted. 'Likely geldings or stallions. Might be we kin get a line on 'em through the hoss traders–' He shook his head. 'No, that ain't likely– You said somethin' about helpin', Dave! Wal, you an' Frank better keep yourselves ready case we need t'git a posse together fast–'

'Why pick on Frank?' Ma demanded, whirling round on Lack. 'He ain't twenty yet, an' besides – he – well, he ain't like Davy here who kin look after himself–'

'Sure, Herb. What Ma says is right. We got

148

enough men in the Valley as can use guns without callin' on – well, men as young as Frank. He ain't even got a gun–'

'He's sure good with a deer rifle,' Walt Dillon murmured. To Frank and Clovis Hervey it was as though a stick of dynamite had been hurled into the room and lay there, its fuse burning in unison to their quickening heartbeats.

Clovis flashed her son a glance from beneath veiled eyes. Frank had stood that blow pretty well! It had rocked him, but neither Herb nor Will were paying him undue attention.

Lack shrugged. 'Wal, et ain't happened yet, Dave. Mebbe we won't need either o' you. But, we don't know yet if them jaspers was workin' alone or if they're members of a bunch–'

'Could be that Wey's bank was no more'n a try-out, Dave,' Fiedler drawled, rolling a quirly and pasting it to his lower lip. 'We gotta be prepared should they try again–'

'You ain't tellin' us a coupla road agents would try robbin' the same bank *twice?*' Frank demanded with well simulated surprise.

Fiedler gave him a look. 'We ain't tryin' to tell you that, Frank, at-all. But the stage is rollin' in next Friday from Belleville an' Sid'll be carryin' a weighty strong-box. We jest nacherally don't want to be caught one-footed again, is all!'

Frank's mouth opened and closed again quickly. *Don't ask too many dam' questions,* he thought.

Again it was brother Dave who, so innocently helped out.

'What about a guard. What about Ed Stubbins–?'

'Guess he'll be ridin' the box alongside Sid as usual,' Lack told them, 'but we sure want to cover all the angles. Sid'll be warned tomorrow to keep his eyes extry peeled on Friday. Likely me an Will'll sashay around some, over to cañon country.

'Anyways,' Lack finished, heaving himself upright with an effort. 'We figgered to give you the news an' if–?'

'I'll be around any time you want,' Dave Hervey replied soberly...

Dave stepped from the saddle, tied the roan's reins and moved with a lithe grace across the threshold.

He smiled at the girl, noting with a pleased wonder the flush of colour in her cheeks, the welcoming sparkle in her emerald eyes. But it was Aaron, behind the counter, who spoke first.

'Mawnin', Dave. How's things at Spanish Creek, huh? Reckon you know Sorrel by now, from what she told me! Come on in, boy, an' quit blockin' out the light!'

Dave moved across the room, wondering, not for the first time, at Sperry's amazing ability to identify folk the moment they stepped into the room.

Dave walked lightly, like a true fighter or hunter; but he wore no jingling spur chains. To Aaron these indications were all he needed to identify the newcomer as Dave Hervey.

On the rare occasions when some stranger dropped in, then, of course, the old frontiersman acted cagey, saying little, letting the other do the talking and weighing up every cadence of voice, every intonation of accent. He could even give a man's height to within an inch by judging the level at which voice issued from throat. He could gauge a man's weight to within a few pounds, entirely by the vibration, strong or weak, caused by his walk.

Dave had been here often enough over the years, but Frank scarce ever. Why, Frank had never believed Dave's talk about old Aaron Sperry; always grinningly accused him of spinning yarns!…

'You heard from Sorrel about the bank raid, I guess, Aaron?'

Sperry nodded, peered through his thick-lensed spectacles. 'Shore was a shock for Sorrel, walkin' into Blessiter's an' finding a couple of men laid out an' the safe cleaned out!'

Dave turned to the girl, 'What did you do next?'

'Why, I guess I just stood there for a few seconds, kinda like I had grown roots!' She laughed now; she could afford to. But it hadn't been so funny at the time!

'It came to me then, that the man I had bumped into – yes we sure did collide with each other! – must have been the bank robber. Well, I ran out on to the street but there wasn't anyone real close just then. I figured the best way to get some action was to yell my head off!'

'You screamed?'

'Enough to wake the dead, I reckon,' she smiled. 'An' it sure produced results. Seemed like the whole town woke up suddenly an' came a-runnin'!

'But of course, by the time the officers had gone inside an' looked around and questioned me on what I knew – well, the robbers were long since out of town!'

Dave nodded thoughtfully, built and fired a smoke. 'Gimme some more baccy an' papers, Aaron, will you?'

'Sure.' Sperry reached unerringly to a shelf, planked a half-pound of smoking mixture and papers in front of Dave.

'I cain't git much outa her about it, Dave,' he grinned, 'but seems like there was a mite o' trouble here when I hadta leave Sorrel alone–'

'Gucht?' Dave looked across at the girl. She moved her head infinitesimally in a negative gesture.

'Yeah! That bucko Munro Gucht's gittin' too big fer his pants,' Sperry growled. 'He–'

'It was nothin', Aaron. 'Twasn't so much Sorrel he was rilin' as me. 'Fraid I lost my durn temper an' took his gun.'

The old man's eyes widened behind the thick lenses. 'You did? Wal, I guess mebbe thet cut the rooster down to size! Ain't many hombres in the Valley as could take Gucht's gun off him an' live to tell the tale. But I'm shore glad yuh showed up, Dave, an' pasted him like Sorrel told me–'

'He'll mebbe come back for his cartridges–'

'He's already done so – Dave,' the girl smiled, silently thanking him with the warmth in her eyes. 'He didn't say anythin'–'

'An' he shore didn't buy nuthin',' Sperry cackled. 'But you better watch it, Dave. Gucht's a killer–'

'Sure, sure. But I'm thinkin' Gucht an' most everyone is busy worryin' over Wildcat's first bank robbery, huh?'

Sperry's myopic gaze lifted to Dave's face.

'That's what I'm gittin at, Dave. Some low polecat like Gucht could burn you down from behind an' mebbe fix things to look like them bank robbers is still around!

Shove the blame on to the man with a rep. It's been done before!'

'It's an angle, an' thanks for the warning,' Dave drawled. 'Now I better get back else Frank'll figure I'm leavin' all the work to him.'

'You are not going without a cup of coffee, *Mr Hervey!*' Sorrel smiled, her full red lips curving the words, a soft light shining in her wide green eyes.

He watched her swing through the doorway leading to the rear rooms, aware that suddenly a bond existed between them. It was as though they shared some special secret unsuspected by anyone else, even by Aaron for all his finely attuned senses.

'Talkin' of Frank,' the trader grunted, stacking goods from a box on to the counter, 'reminds me! Ain't often your brother hits this trail, Dave–'

'He came by here?' Hervey was surprised.

'Not only came by, he dropped in an' made some purchases. Mebbe we lost one customer an' gained another!' Sperry grinned.

Dave was puzzled. For one thing, Frank had said nothing about stopping off at the Trading Post and in any case it didn't lie on the trail to Caprock.

And what in tarnation would Frank be wanting here that he couldn't buy at Wildcat or the trail town itself? He didn't use

154

tobacco and he had made his several purchases at Caprock. He had said so! Shirt, hat, Ma's clock—

It was not in Dave Hervey's nature to pry into other folks' affairs, but the family had always shared things; even seemingly insignificant items of news. If Frank had wanted to ride out to Sperry's for some reason, why hadn't he mentioned it? He could have gone even if it had meant skipping a few chores!

'When was this, Aaron?' Dave found himself voicing the question almost without realizing it.

'When was what? Oh! you mean Frank's visit, huh! Lemme see – I guess it musta been last week sometime. Why, sure, it was the very day Sorrel arrived, come to think of it. Was jest fixin' to hitch up the team and drive in to meet the stage. Guess that makes it the Sunday o' last week. Most allus open on a Sunday, leastways, when the weather's fine–'

Dave thought, *Frank was cutting out that dozen steers from the breaks; the bunch I hazed to Caprock on Monday–*

'Hope you found the dye took all right, Dave? Sure is good fer stainin' leather–'

'Dye?'

Sperry glanced up from the account book he had been going through.

'Sure. The black stain Frank bought; a coupla gallon jars! Ain't the kind o' merchandise many traders carry, but every fall-time, I git a bunch o' Navahoes–'

'Oh, sure,' Dave drawled. 'The black dye! Yeah, I guess it's good stuff, Aaron, like you say. I–'

The rear door swung open and Sorrel entered, a tray in her hands.

'You excuse me now, Dave. I got some book work–'

'I was just goin' to suggest settin' on the porch,' Sorrel smiled, moving on through the doorway and placing the tray on an up-turned box. Hervey followed her outside.

'How do you like it – Dave?'

'Thick an' sweet, Sorrel,' he grinned, lowering himself into a chair under the ramada.

He felt slightly guilty at sitting here idling away the morning. Guilty, too, that he should be probing the mystery of the jars of dye. Hell! There was a simple enough explanation if he but knew. About time he quit the business of riding herd on his kid brother!

'Go ahaid an' smoke if you want,' the red-haired girl invited.

He grinned sheepishly. 'I'm sorry, I guess I was thinkin'–'

'That, Mr Hervey,' she smiled, 'was absolutely obvious!'

There was no hint of censure in her tone for his seeming ill-manners and now, looking at her sitting no more than six feet away, he forgot about Frank's purchases.

He could see that the beauty of her eyes was not alone in their startlingly unusual colour, for thick lashes outlined them strongly. Her nose was short, wide at the nostrils and the long upper lip merged into a generously full mouth.

He noted with a start that she had changed from the grey working dress into a green one, similar to that which she had been wearing when Gucht had–

But this was shot with red-gold, *bay-colour*, Dave thought. It seemed to be on fire with her slightest movement, especially the tight, low-cut corsage.

She coloured, yet secretly amused in the sure knowledge that Dave Hervey's searching glance did not possess the unpleasant brashness of Munro Gucht's!

'I guess I haven't gotten over the shock of meeting a real bandit, yet.'

The flippant tone was partially belied by her sober expression. Dave had not previously considered this aspect of the encounter, but now he nodded.

'Reckon it's the kind of experience you start thinkin' about later on. At the time, why, I guess there's all the excitement – it don't give you time to think or feel–'

'That's right enough, Dave. Oh, I guess I was angry first an' then scared some, but everything happened so fast. And then the sheriff started in poundin' me with questions. Was he dark or fair? What colour eyes? Bearded? How tall? Approximate weight? – Why, for goodness sake! I only caught a glimpse, no more'n a second or two, I guess, before he turned and disappeared round the corner!'

'Reckon he didn't even apologize, huh?'

'Not likely! He was too mean and – and ill-bred. For just a moment we stared back at each other. I couldn't see his face clearly, the hat brim shaded his eyes, but they were kind of glittering like – like a snake's–'

'You didn't have time to take in what he was wearin', the kind o' clothes–?'

She shook her head slowly, thoughtfully. 'I couldn't really swear to anythin', Dave. That's what I told the law officers, but they didn't seem to believe me, especially the fat one, the sheriff!'

Dave smiled. 'Don't take any notice of Herb Lack. He's allus a bit pompous; made that way, I guess. But Will Fiedler now, he's different an' plenty smart I'd judge, though up till now there's been little enough crime around these parts.'

Sorrel finished her coffee and pushed the cup to one side, leaning back in the chair, closing her eyes for a moment.

'Lack sure riled me,' she said, 'droppin' hints about citizens not co-operatin' with the law! Maybe it's wrong to say this, but I wouldn't tell him anythin' now, even if I *had* remembered one or two things!'

'You *have* remembered something, haven't you, Sorrel?'

'I don't mind telling *you,* that several things have come back to me. I honestly didn't recall them at the time, but–'

'It can happen like that, I reckon. You git jumped on right away an' your mind goes kinda blank. You sure cain't remember a thing, 'specially if some smartie like Herb's shootin' questions at you right, left an' centre!'

'Sure. That's the way it was. But Saturday evening and again yesterday, I went back over the whole thing, from the time I drove up in the wagon–'

'Tell me from the beginning, Sorrel.'

He thought, *to hell with worryin' over the wagon-shed door!*

CHAPTER 11

ONCE IN A LIFETIME

'Well, Aaron wanted to cache my jewellery and some *dinero* at the bank. He was pretty busy checkin' off some goods he hauled back from Stella; puttin' up new orders he'd drummed up; that kind o' thing. So I took the wagon an' drove into Wildcat. Guess it was around two when I pulled up outside the bank. And here's somethin' I remembered later! It was seein' the two blacks standin' near the corner of East and Main. One had a rider atop; the other horse must've belonged to the actual robber, though, of course, I had no idea–'

'You couldn't describe the hosses or the waitin' rider?'

She shook her head. 'Only like I said, they were blacks, I think, and – and I *think* they had white stockings but it's no good taking that for gospel! As to the slim one' – again the headshake– 'his back was towards me and I didn't really *look–*'

'This isn't evidence to be used in court,' Dave smiled. 'It's just your *impressions* I'm interested in.'

'Well, I pulled in a few yards farther up, on account I overshot the bank. I was looking down to see I had my reticule and the bag we had slipped the jewels into. That's how it was I didn't see him until it was too late!

'Guess I was feeling pretty mad–'

'Why not?' Dave drawled. 'You got red hair!'

Her eyelids drew together until the lashes formed dark curtains before two fires of green. As suddenly, her simulated anger vanished and to Dave, the sound of her

160

laughter was like the golden peal of bells at a Spanish *fiesta*.

'Yesterday,' she continued, watching him build a smoke, 'it seemed like I could see that face a mite clearer. Dark eyes set kinda close together, a lean face, black with stubble. Mebbe that's just somethin' I conjured up since,' she admitted. 'I sure wouldn't care to swear on it. But he did have a tight, mean mouth! Reckon that's somethin' a woman notices – a man's mouth–' She stopped suddenly, blushing furiously, and then hurried on.

'I – I mean it wasn't so hidden like when a man is wearing a full beard or an unwaxed moustache–'

'You recollect anything about his duds, like hat or shirt, f'r instance?'

She moistened her lips, frowning in concentration.

'It was a low-crowned stetson, I reckon, Dave. But nothin' special that I can call to mind. Not even the colour. I got the idea there was a bandana around his neck, like any puncher might wear and a darkish shirt. I sure don't remember anything outstanding, it was all so – so – well, *neutral*, I guess you'd call it!'

'Well, Sorrel, thet's a pretty durn good description anyway you look at it, considerin' you had only a few moments. How about height? You say the man waitin' with

161

the hosses was small an' slim, well, how did *this* hombre compare?'

'Why, taller an' bigger than his partner, I reckon, but no more'n just above your shoulders I'd say.

'Ain't much use askin' me about weight,' she smiled. 'I cain't ever guess–'

'What d'you figger I go?'

She thought a while and this time it was Dave who had to subject himself to a searching scrutiny.

'I – well it's only a wild guess, but I'd say somewhere around – huh – one hun'ed an' sixty? Is that anywhere near?'

'Not bad, *chiquita!* Nearer a hun'ed an' eighty in fact. Well, what does that make the bandit! Mebbe one-sixty?'

She shook her head so vigorously that the black velvet ribbon slipped, releasing her hair in a red-gold stream to fall on softly rounded shoulders.

'He was considerably smaller than you, Dave! Don't forget I said height about your shoulder level or a little above – why, I guess he'd be about my height–'

'Stand up,' Hervey said getting to his feet.

She arose from the chair moving to within a yard of where Dave stood.

He caught her bared shoulders in his hard grip. Yet there was a rough gentleness about him and she had no wish to draw away.

'Cain't see if you're up to my shoulders or

162

not, less'n you stand right close – like this!'

He pulled her near, trying to figure whether she wanted it this way.

Her face was raised now and her eyes searched his face.

'Do you figure he was taller or shorter'n me, Dave?' Her voice husked a little as her hands gripped the lapels of his coat and almost diffidently slid to behind his neck.

He saw the sober promise in her smoky eyes and bent to kiss her, drawing back sharply as Aaron's footsteps sounded across the room beyond.

'Reckon mebbe somewheres around your height, Sorrel,' he smiled, 'but I ain't certain sure until we put it to the test!'

He was building a cigarette when Aaron came out.

'Thanks for the coffee,' he told them. 'Reckon I'll be on my way—'

'Drop in any time, Dave!' the oldster invited. 'Allus glad to see you. Reckon you're company fer Sorrel, too.'

'Am I?' he asked her.

She nodded and smiled and Dave turned and unhitched the buckskin's reins.

He stood there a moment, booted left foot in the oxbow, looking down at a black smear on the brown leather saddle.

'I'd say it was around five-foot seven or eight, Dave,' she whispered, 'but if you wanna make sure some other time, why I

163

guess I jest nacherally am a law-abiding citizen who wants to see the ends of justice served!'

'I'll take you up on that, Sorrel,' he said, but his voice was oddly quiet.

He looked back once, but he was too far away for the smiling girl to see the hardening of his jaw and the bleak expression in his grey eyes...

'Where you bin, Frank?' Dave's voice was unaccountably sharp, hauling Frank up as he made for the barns.

'Lookin' after *yore* cattle, mister,' Frank snapped. 'What makes you so all-fired interested seein' as you bin away all mawnin'?'

Dave shrugged and turned away. This was no time for a row or a show-down. Besides, he wasn't sure enough. Not by a heck of a jugful! In fact now, the more he thought about his grinding suspicions and the way small things had dovetailed so neatly, the more he despised himself with a sick revulsion and loathing.

Frank gazed after his brother wonderingly. Had he found out anything? He was sure on the prod an' even Ma had been actin' queer since yesterday!

Or was he dreaming it all up? he wondered. Maybe he was getting what a guy once called 'sensitive to atmosphere'.

He gigged the buckskin into the barn,

164

stripped off the rig and forked feed into the manger. Thoughtfully pausing every so often, he rubbed the animal down until the buckskin's coat shone like new satin.

That was another funny thing, Dave hadn't seemed to notice he'd been riding the buckskin again. Mostly, brother Dave was fussy some, about anyone taking either of the cow ponies without a by-your-leave. The hell with worrying what Dave knew! It couldn't be much if anything, else he would surely come right out with it. So would Ma, Frank figured. Ma wasn't the kind of woman to hold back when she reckoned there was something needed saying.

But, maybe in Ma's case, it was the thought of becoming Mrs Dillon; it could give her a queer feeling to realize that in a few weeks maybe, she would be having a husband for the first time in years. Come to think of it, Ma hadn't talked much about it and neither had Dave, but – Frank moved to the open doorway, stood looking out across the yard towards the house. He was determined on one thing and that was, *neither Ma nor Dave was going to stop him pulling off this next job!*

He hadn't reckoned on another one so soon; not until the heat had cooled. But this was too good a chance to pass up. This was the kind of gift which only comes once in a lifetime when Johnny Law rides along and *tells* you most all the things you want to know!

Frank pulled a flask from his pocket, took a long pull and reflected on what a smart idea it had been, arranging for Emma to be at the arroyo every day at noon, just in case.

By riding out soon after Dave this morning, he had been able to rendezvous with the waiting girl and outline his plans...

The first thing that struck Frank as he kneed the buckskin into the arroyo was the startling change in Emma's appearance. A transformation, the sight of which sent waves of anger coursing through his body. The little fool! Hadn't she any better sense than to rig herself out like a doll on a Christmas tree?

He reined in, stared at her standing there as pleased as all get-out, exhaling cigarette smoke from her thin nostrils.

'Why don't you hang out a sign, Emma, just in case someone don't know you next time?'

Her black eyes smouldered. She dropped the quirly and trod on it with savage force.

'I ridden round this neck o' the woods better'n a week,' she spat, 'an ain't nobody seen me yet, nor will, ef'n I got a mind they shouldn't!'

He studied her for a long moment. By general standards what he saw was a great improvement, yet a dangerous one. For dressed like that, she could be picked out a mile away; could scarce fail to attract attention. Perhaps she hoped to kindle some man's interest, Frank thought. Well, okay, but *after* they had cleaned up, not *before*!

Her short black hair was topped by a white stetson pushed well back. A dazzling vermilion scarf encircled her bronzed throat, setting off the brilliant blue silk shirt. The fringes of a long, deerhide skirt touched the top of hand-tooled Justins on which were strapped big sunflower spurs of silver.

Frank saw that the gun-belt also was new, twin holstered and carrying two ivory-handled guns. *She musta spent close to five hundred bucks,* he thought with a contemptuous sneer, and suddenly recollected that he too was fixing to rig himself out in more fancy clothes.

Moreover, if it had not been for this strange, unattached girl, Blessiter's most likely could not have been raided; leastways not for a long time and *he* would not be so well off by some fifteen hundred dollars.

His mood changed and as he stepped from the saddle the girl's hard face flushed with pleasure before his warmly approving glance.

'Listen, Emma! I ain't got much time now but you be here around noon day after tomorrow, like we fixed it last time—'

'Yuh ain't figgerin' the heat's cooled – not after what yuh said about that Fiedler gent?'

Frank shook his head. 'We still got to go careful, but Lack an' Fiedler rode over yesterday *an' dished it all out on a plate!*'

Her eyes glittered excitedly. 'How?'

Quickly he told her about the stage schedule for Friday; what Sid Machoff and Ed Stubbins would be carrying.

'It's tailor-made fer us,' he finished. 'We'd be crazy to pass up such a chance–'

'Once in a lifetime, I guess, that them bustard law-dogs spill the grazy like that!' She held her gaze on him for a while, thinking the thing out.

'Yuh considered, Frank,' she said shortly, 'it *could* be a trap! Supposin' them officers had a hunch yuh was on the bank job an' they figgered to spread a little salt on our tails; sell us a bum steer–?'

'Bait the trap with information about Friday's gold shipment, huh?' He was startled by the idea for a second, then quickly shook his head, grinning.

'It was a clean job, Emma, an' we left no string untied. If you're wantin' *proof* that we foxed 'em, it's this! *They wouldn't 've told us they was fixin' to take a* pasear *near the cañons if they was settin' a trap!*

'The stage road from Belleville drops down through cañon country an' that's where we'll be come Friday. No, Emma! If

Lack an' Fiedler was suspicious they sure wouldn't tip me off *they* was plannin' to be there!'

She rolled another quirly, wiped a match alight and trickled smoke out over her thin lips.

'Thet makes sense, I reckon. But I been thinkin' around the dame yuh knocked into. Who was she, Frank?'

He had been waiting for the question and was able to hedge convincingly. 'Never set eyes on her before, like I said, an' I guess that means she ain't ever seen me, either!'

But he was desperately worried about the Sperry girl and impatient to be free from Emma's probing questions...

Throughout the ride back to Spanish Creek, Frank Hervey chewed over the problem of Sorrel Sperry. Had the girl really given Lack and Fiedler no more than a vague description, or were the law men playing it close to the vest?

There was another angle, too, and equally dangerous. That was Dave's friendship with her. Supposing for some reason, Dave started in talking about his kid brother, even to the extent of describing him? Or worse still, what if he invited the dame out here to meet the family and they came face to face!

Frank told himself that Sorrel Sperry *couldn't* identify him. His face had been darkened with stain to give a beard-stubbled impression, his hat had been pulled well down and the whole incident could not have lasted over two-three seconds.

Despite his own arguments to the contrary, Frank began to feel the first tentative chill breath of impending disaster...

Dave dropped his hat on to the wall antlers, set himself down at the spotlessly spread table as Ma came in carrying a tray of plates and dishes.

She gave him a quick, anxious kind of smile, her glance flickering across to the hat stand and back to the empty chair.

'Figgered I heard Frank ride out soon after you this mawnin', Dave.'

He nodded, passed vegetables across to his mother and then mechanically piled his own plate. He ate, not with any great appetite but to refuel his tired body.

Work had been extra heavy this week what with all the branding and Frank away part of Wednesday and now again today.

He said, choosing his words carefully: 'Claimed he wanted to bank the money he got for grub-stakin' the fella in Caprock. Said it was kinda dangerous leavin' five hun'ed bucks lyin' around a place like this.'

'Four hun'ed, Dave,' Ma said quietly. 'He gave me five double eagles!'

Dave stared. This was the first he had

heard of Frank's generosity; pity, shame, contempt ran through him as he thought how Frank's recent actions were merely serving to confirm the terrible, growing suspicion.

Yet, love was there in Dave's breast, so strong, that he began to wonder which side he would take if–

'So a Hervey has at last gotten himself a real bank account in town?' Ma said, making no more than a half-hearted attempt to eat.

'Well, not in town, Ma. Frank's caching his *dinero* at the Cattlemen's an' Stockmen's bank in Caprock–'

'Why ever?'

'Like he reminded me,' Dave smiled wryly, 'Blessiter's bin robbed! Frank don't figger it's so safe any more.'

Ma nodded. 'Of course. I almost forgot. Reckon it's been a hectic kinda week–' She paused, trying to sort out her jumbled thoughts into some kind of order. Frank was her main concern. *What was he up to today?* she wondered. *Had he really gone to Caprock as he had said or was he even now stealing other folks' cattle, tangling with another Hatchet rider?*

But, there was also the very real problem of Walt and their forthcoming marriage. The fact that she had accepted Dillon, in order to save Frank from a hanging, did not make

171

the prospect of sharing the cattleman's life at Hatchet any the more entrancing! On the contrary, Ma could not help thinking about the Mex girl, Rosita Morales. Maybe it was just malicious gossip; maybe there was fire under the smoke!

She forced herself to assume at least an outward appearance of cheerfulness, bustling back with dishes, smilingly returning with heaped plates of pie and cream, even as she thought: *What guarantee have I that Walt will not talk once he has married me?...*

Dave, as unaware of Ma's problem as she was of his, found his mind constantly harking back to the question: *could Frank really be one of the bank robbers, terrible as the very idea seemed?*

Undeniably Aaron Sperry had served the kid with large quantities of black dye and some bleach and it was likely that Frank figured old Sperry would not recognise him. Why had he behaved so secretively if he had nothing to hide?

Dave thought of the black mark on his saddle. Frank had taken the buckskin and the Walker saddle last Saturday when he had supposedly spent the day in Caprock. But Dave had examined that black smudge again and was prepared to swear it was a spirit dye stain!

He thought also of Sorrel's description, a far more complete picture than she had

172

painted for Lack and it could well fit Frank!

Yet, if this were all true – and Dave fervently prayed that he was wrong – then, who was the small, slimly built second man?

He could think of no one in the valley who really fitted the description; no one at least possessing such a combination of criminal instincts and cold nerve.

Moreover, Sorrel had seen the bandits' horses and swore they were blacks with white stockings–

Well, if Frank *had* spent Saturday in Caprock it should be easy enough to prove. Apart from having bought Ma's clock and a few new duds for himself, he would certainly have been seen around the town. Men like Marshal Hockin, the hostler, saloon and store-keepers, *they* would know!

Dave pushed his plate aside, smiled his thanks as Ma poured fresh coffee.

'We ain't had much chance to talk about you an' Walt.'

Clovis Hervey laughed. 'Guess when you git as old as Walt an' me, Dave, there ain't the excitement an' plumb foolishness as when a young girl gits wed to a handsome boy!'

'Mebbe not. But I still ain't certain you're doin' the right thing.

'Sure, Dillon's got money, but like you said, it ain't everythin'. The important thing is, are you goin' to be happy? I ain't sayin'

173

it's wildly excitin' here, Ma, lookin' after us an'–'

'I don't seek for wild excitement, Dave. Mebbe I did once, but that was a long time ago.

'As for lookin' after you two, why, I guess that's my idea of happiness–' Her voice shook and Dave saw the tears start in her eyes.

'You don't *haveta* marry Walt,' he said roughly. 'You can call it off any time you want. If you figger Frank an' me'll get along better without – Hell, Ma! We want you to have somethin' in life, better'n this' – he indicated the room, the whole section with a sweep of his arm – 'but that don't mean–'

'I know exactly what you're tryin' to say, Dave, an' I thank the good Lord for it!' She blinked the wetness from her eyes and smiled in a way that partially, at least, removed his doubts and fears for her well-being.

'I'm goin' to finish the wagon-shed door,' he told her presently, when the remains of the meal had been cleared away.

He reached for his hat as Ma's voice held him in mid-stride.

'Wh – where did Frank go on Wednesday, Dave? He didn't say–'

Dave looked at her steadily, then gave his easy smile.

'Told me he aimed to pay Charlie Schwarz

the two bucks he owed him.'

She smiled brightly as Dave turned and stepped outside.

When she heard him cross the yard towards the barns, she stopped smiling, thinking back to Wednesday, when she had glimpsed Frank riding off, not north-east towards Wildcat, but headed for the broken country north-west...

CHAPTER 12

STAGE COACH TO WILDCAT

Sid Machoff held the ribbons easily in his big, sun-blackened hands, as his gaze flickered over the semi-arid country.

His jaws moved ceaselessly and from time to time he shot a thin stream of tobacco juice from the corner of his mouth. The stage swayed and bumped perilously over the high cañon trail, occasionally throwing the few occupants inside from their seats.

Sid knew he was making it rough for them, but he was altogether anxious to reach Wildcat safely and on schedule.

If the sheriff hadn't been so all-fired jumpy on Monday, warning him and Ed to keep their eyes peeled, he wouldn't now be even *thinking* of road-agents and worrying over the strong-box at his feet.

Irritated somewhat by Ed Stubbins's complete unconcern, Sid jabbed an elbow in his ribs causing the guard to jerk upright in his seat and clutch one-handedly at the rail.

'Whassamatter, Sid? You aimin' to git me killed or sump'n? Why, we ain't even in sight o' town–'

'Sure, Ed. We got another ten miles yet, but Lack and Fiedler claimed–'

'Oh, *that!*' Stubbins laughed, shifted the shot-gun more comfortably on to his knees. 'Reckon we musta hauled this yer box a fair number o' times, Sid, over the last three-four years, huh?'

'Yeah. We shore have, Ed.'

'An' I don't ever remember anythin' happenin' to it! Jest because a couple saddle-bums drifted into town an' stuck up Bles–'

Crack! A gun barked close at hand and a bullet screamed by even closer, missing Ed's head by a hand's-breadth. A harsh voice sounded its warning as the stage-coach men found themselves staring into the eyes of two masked riders!

The thing had happened with such incredible suddenness, the ambush spot so well chosen, that it almost seemed as though the riders had materialized out of thin air.

It was only afterwards that Machoff realized how cleverly the road-agents had made use of the scant cover along this stretch of the trail. They had deliberately chanced their arm here, figuring that even if the driver and guard *were* on the look-out for trouble, they would be anticipating it farther along where the trail dropped down between towering walls of rock!

But, for all his previous unconcern and sceptical outlook, Ed Stubbins was a good man to have around. This was not the first time, by a jugful, that Ed had been called on to act and think fast, especially during Indian trouble.

He acted fast now, swinging the shot-gun round despite the fact that one of the riders still held a smoking six-gun on the coach. As for Sid, his hands were too full handling the six-horse team to be able to give Ed any assistance.

Quick as Stubbins was, his only real chance lay in another near miss by the gun-handy bandit. He couldn't hope to beat a gun already pointed at him, but a quick anger and determination not to let these men get the better of him, led to Ed's undoing.

His forefinger was half-way through the trigger-guard when a six-gun slug caught him full in the chest. Sid Machoff had slammed down a boot on to the brake lever and now shock held him stiff as he watched Ed keel over, face an agonized mask of sweat, big hands, empty of shotgun, clutched to his chest.

Machoff was no tender-stomached weakling. He had seen men die worse than Ed. But he and Stubbins had tooled Butterworth, Lovington and Wells Fargo coaches all over the place and had continued their double-act for the Brown and Lacey Lines who operated the Belleville-Wildcat trail.

Machoff felt sick, not so much physically as mentally. He knew as Ed's body bounced off the whipple-trees to crash in the dust, his own life was not worth a plugged nickel. Once a road-agent had killed, he didn't hesitate a second or third time if danger threatened!

There was just a slim chance, Machoff thought, that if he did like he was told, he *might* get away in one piece.

If he could give a good description, spot some give-away characteristic–

'Throw down thet box an' don't touch yore gun!' The same man who had snarled at them before, issued the ultimatum in a hoarse voice, muffled by the concealing bandana.

The smaller of the two men, Machoff noticed, had quickly spurred forward to cover the coach's occupants, two of whom were staring from the window in fixed-eyed horror.

'*Git movin'*, *dam' you!*' As the words were uttered a Colt flew into the robber's left hand and a slug slammed into the box inches from Machoff's left leg.

Hurriedly, but carefully, the driver reached down, tugged at one of the leather handles and heaved the box up on end, letting it slowly keel until, like Ed's body a moment ago, it crashed down into the dust a few yards clear of the coach.

Again, Sid was hard put to hold the restive, prancing horses, even though the brake was on. But Machoff had not wasted opportunities during his few seconds' respite. He had first off, marked the horses as big roan geldings, not blacks as he would have figured. But they both had four white stockings and the riders atop were certainly slight men, one scarcely bigger than a school kid!

Machoff could see nothing of their faces under the dark bandanas and pulled down stetsons, but he did notice pearl- and ivory-handled guns and shining new belts. Also, his narrowed gaze had taken in the carbine stocks at the saddle-fenders of both riders.

'*Hold them hosses an' shuck yore gun! One wrong move, mister–*'

But Sid permitted himself no sudden, brash actions, as he slowly withdrew his open weapon and threw it to the ground.

The other bandit, having collected a

couple of hand guns from inside the coach, now moved around and slid from the saddle, gun in one hand and empty sack in the other.

He stood some five or six feet from the strong-box and sent a succession of rapid and accurately aimed shots at the lock. Quickly he replaced the empty gun and drew the other one, holding it in preparedness as he bent down and commenced transferring mail packages as well as gold pokes and bills to the sack.

It was then that Machoff, from his high perch atop the box, received a shock which jolted him perhaps even more than Ed's death had done.

It was so crazy that for a moment, Sid figured he was going funny in the head!

The man's red scarf had slipped a little, revealing not only a bronzed neck and chest, but—

Machoff blinked and swore softly, holding himself still, conscious of the fact that he was covered by the other bandit's gun.

He stole another glance and, when the unmounted, masked figure leaned forward for the last handful of money, Machoff knew that he had not been mistaken. *The smaller of these two road agents was a woman!*

He had little time to reflect on his discovery, or to consider what value lay in it, if any.

The 'girl' as he now knew her to be, moved up quickly to the team and without warning, shot the two leaders through the head!

In the ensuing uproar, Sid again found himself with a fight on his hands. The two leaders were dead in their traces, but the remaining four, foam-flecked and frightened, nickered shrilly, pawing the dust and side-stepping in a futile effort to avoid the smell of death so close in front of them. Futile, because Sid Machoff was always the master.

The girl's hard gaze was on him now, the smoking gun dangling from her gloved right hand. If Machoff could have had his gun, fought it out with them even with odds of two to one, he would not have felt the fear which crawled over him now and touched his back and neck and forehead until the sweat stood out in glistening drops cold as ice.

It was as though he could *see* her brain working coolly and cold-bloodedly, considering whether it was necessary for him too, to die.

A man's voice, pitched high with fear, sounded from the coach and the girl whirled, gun raised.

'Hold et, you fool!' It was the other bandit, who had again raised his voice, and as the girl hesitated, then slid the gun slowly back

into leather, Machoff let go his breath in a deep, juddering sigh.

'We don't want no more killin's,' the man continued in a quieter tone, gigging his roan forward and scooping up the money sack from where it lay. 'Let's git the hell outa here!'

Wordlessly, she caught up her mount's trailing reins. She had one boot in the stirrup when the sudden rataplan of racing hooves burst on the air, urgent, violent–

For a split second, the principal actors in the drama of murder and robbery remained poised in mid-act. Then almost instantly, gazes swung round, narrowed and focused on the rider hurtling towards them from a fissure where the rock walls lifted some mile or so farther along the trail.

Echo and reverberation around the caprock must have been responsible for creating the impression that horse and rider were so close. Yet even though there had been over a mile of open ground to cover, the racing horseman was already within carbine range. In a few more seconds it would be possible for a good shot to take him with a six-gun!

Sid Machoff kept himself still. His gaze swung from the oncoming rider to the girl, now astride her mount.

A moment ago, he had told himself that help was at hand. But a strong uneasiness had stirred in him as several things became apparent simultaneously.

Instead of lighting out *pronto* the bandits were holding their eager mounts on a tight rein, evidently prepared to deal with this new situation first. And, at the same moment that the stage-driver recognized the racing horse and its rider, a man's voice screamed out: *'Don't shoot! – it's my–'*

Machoff exploded into action as Dave Hervey leaped from the faltering buckskin, rolled over on the ground and somehow or another, regained his feet.

Amidst the noise and confusion, Sid had not heard the sound of that shot, but his eyes were on the smoking pistol in the girl's hand. She had shot Dave Hervey's horse from under him and was now cold-bloodedly cocking the gun as Dave began walking slowly forward.

It musta bin the other guy who shouted, Machoff thought as he scooped up Ed's shot-gun from the floor and flung himself from the box on to the road.

He was only just in time for a bullet screamed over his head, ricochetting off the iron arm of the box where he had been seated a second or two before.

He scrambled to his feet, managing to reach the rear of the coach in spite of a twisted ankle.

He lifted the shot-gun as the girl fired at

Dave Hervey.

She couldn't have missed killing at such close range if her roan had not swung round. As it was, that slight movement probably saved Dave's life. The slug furrowed the side of his head, a creasing wound, instead of a fatal one.

But, by the same token, Machoff's load of buckshot missed its mark.

He fired both barrels at once and cursed bitterly, the masked girl and her companion remaining apparently unscathed.

She was the first to wheel, urging the other rider forward with a quick sweep of her gun arm. For a moment, it seemed as though he would ignore her imperative action, loath to leave, staring back as he was at Hervey lying on the ground.

Still cursing, half-sobbing in angry frustration, Machoff hobbled round to the exposed side of the coach, reaching down for his own six-gun to where it had dropped in the dust.

He took careful aim and fired. The hammer dropped with a click. The gun was choked with dirt. He flung the useless weapon away and dived for the gun still in the dead guard's holster.

The girl had turned in the saddle and straight away the pair put their mounts to a gallop. Even as Machoff fired, he knew that they were now beyond six-gun range.

Slowly, he dropped Ed's gun into his own holster, watching until the racing bandits became lost from view.

Then he turned and began walking across to Dave Hervey, heedless of the sudden babble of shrill voices from the coach's interior...

When Dave had walked across to the wagon-shed, it had been with every intention of trying to shake off this desperate worry, through hard, physical work.

But the thing would not leave him and added to this was the dawning realization that all was not well with Ma!

Was it just that she was worked up about her forthcoming marriage and the fact that she would be leaving Pa's home and Pa's section? Or, Dave wondered, *was it that she knew something about Frank?*

He gazed at the half-finished door, not seeing it, and suddenly determined to find the answer he needed by action.

He would not question Ma, because if she knew anything at all, it was up to her whether she talked, and lately her only references to Frank had been either oblique or the penny-plain variety.

Dave threw down the hammer and strode into the stable. He had let Frank take the roan this morning and, wasting no further time in speculation, he flung blanket, saddle and bridle on the gleaming buckskin, led the animal out across the yard and called to Ma through the screen door.

'You'll be all right, Ma? We need some more nails an'–'

She pushed open the door, smiling and nodded. 'Sure, Dave. Where you goin', Wildcat or Sperry's?'

'Reckon I'll haveta try Sperry's or even Caprock, but I ain't aimin' to be late. What's the time now?'

Dave figured it was around one o'clock by the sun and the fact that dinner was invariably at noon.

'It's ten minutes of one, Dave. You got plenty o' time!'

He nodded, stepped into the saddle and lifted his hand as he headed the buckskin out and across the creek.

Dave Hervey was a born rider, and, once clear of the house, he leaned forward low in the saddle, distributing his weight as much for the gelding's benefit as his own.

He held to a gallop, shortly slowed to a steady lope. By continuing this method and by making use of cut-offs, he was able to reach the broken country north-west in fast time and with a comparatively fresh horse under him.

He by-passed the Trading Post by several miles, heading straight for Caprock. And, as he rode, he tried to remember every piece of information Lack and Fiedler had dropped concerning the stage coach run today from Belleville to Wildcat.

But, as far as he could recall now, the law men had not really told them anything that was not common knowledge. Everyone knew the schedules – Mondays and Fridays – with an occasional shorter run on Sundays from the railhead at Caprock.

Dave knew that the stage's scheduled arrival time in Wildcat was around five o'clock in the afternoon. But with Sid Machoff on the box and his slick handling of a team, they might well appear in town a half-hour, even an hour, ahead of schedule. The object of this being to furnish Sid – and Ed, when he was along – with more time in which to down a few drinks.

Allowing then for Sid's ability to coax more from the horses than any of Brown and Lacey's other drivers, the coach *might* roll in as early as four; unlikely perhaps but a possibility.

That meant, Dave thought, as he turned on to Caprock's Main, Machoff could be tooling down the cañon stretch at three-thirty or three-forty-five!

It did not allow much time now, but what Hervey had in mind would likely not take long, distasteful though it was.

Hating the task, Dave unshipped outside the marshal's office, racked his horse and stepped inside.

Marshal Cal Hockin glanced up from a paper-littered desk, frowned and then, recognizing Hervey as the man from Spanish Creek, waved him to a chair.

In a moment or two, Hockin sat back and surveyed his visitor speculatively.

'You're Dave Hervey! You an' your ma run the Spanish Creek section below Crooked River!'

Dave nodded. 'Frank helps us. My younger brother–'

'Oh, yeah, sure. I remember now! Well, Mr Hervey, what is it you're after; anythin' I can do?'

Dave rolled and lit a quirly, pushing sack and papers towards the law man. He schooled himself to appear relaxed and easy.

'Ain't nothin' much, Marshal,' he smiled. 'Fact is, I feel kinda guilty takin' up your time. It's just that Frank an' me had a little argument the other day, coupla weeks back to be exact.

'Y'see,' Dave went on confidentially, 'Frank's only a kid really and needs a bit of watching when it comes to liquor. Well, didn't seem like he was takin' much notice of me tellin' him not to overdo it an' two-three times over the last month, well–' Dave spread his hands.

'You mean he came home liquored up an'

188

left you to do all the work?' Hockin grinned. 'Still an' all, Hervey, it ain't a crime so long as he don't misbehave—'

'Sure, I know. But this is the point. I figgered that Frank needed some *encouragement,* y'see, an' I bet him fifty bucks he couldn't go three weeks without a drink!'

'Go on!'

'Well, it looked like I might be losing myself fifty dollars faster an' I could earn it, because he sure *seemed* to have turned over a new leaf. That is, up until – lemme see – last Saturday it was!

'He was supposed to be ridin' up here, on account he aimed to buy a few things—'

'Last Saturday, you said?' Hockin screwed up his eyes, dragged on the cigarette he had built. 'Why, that was the day Blessiter's bank was robbed. Had notice of it that same evenin' an' the sheriff sent a description—'

Dave nodded, finding a sudden difficulty in breathing easily. He gazed at the tip of his quirly, watching the smoke rise and whip away as it caught the slight breeze from the door.

'Here's what, Marshal! I had to ride to Stella, an' I swear I saw my brother go into the Longhorn saloon there, right on Main! Sure, I was some way off, mebbe three-four hundred yards. I *could* 'a' bin mistaken. When I came up, there was no Hervey hoss at the rack, but I still felt sure—'

'You go in the saloon?'

Dave nodded. 'Sure. An' the funny thing was, a fella *had* been in a moment or two before who was either Frank himself or so dam' near like him–'

'What time of day you figure it was?'

Dave hesitated. 'Why – I – well I guess as near as I kin judge around mid-afternoon, mebbe a little later.'

Hockin smiled. Though he was a tough enough law man to handle the kind of trouble inseparable from any trail town, he was a kindly man and the human side of Hervey's little story touched him with a tolerant amusement.

He could well visualize the set-up and, having seen Hervey's younger brother on several occasions, including last Saturday, deemed it more than likely that the boy gave a little trouble from time to time.

'I can put your mind at ease, Hervey,' the marshal grinned, getting to his feet. 'But it's sure gonna cost you fifty bucks!

'Your brother was sure here in Caprock last Saturday, wanderin' about some; didn't see him my own self 'till an hour or so before dusk, but his hoss was on the street since early mornin'. Was gittin' worried about the animal – with the sun climbin', but along about four or five o'clock, he showed up again an' took it to the livery! Thet same buckskin as is standin' hitched outside right now!'

Hockin shook his head. 'Sorry, Hervey, but you either saw Frank's double in Stella, else it's *you* had oughta do less drinkin'!'…

CHAPTER 13

TIGHTER DRAWS THE NET

Dave emerged from the office in a worse frame of mind than before. What, he asked himself, had he hoped to prove by spinning that yarn? Sure, Frank had fixed himself with a dandy enough alibi that at first inspection appeared to be unshakable.

But despite what the marshal had told him, he felt certain that if he were to make the rounds of Caprock questioning saloon- and store-keepers, Frank's carefully built alibi would collapse as easily as a house of cards! In any case, if he were to carry out the second part of his plan, there was no time to lose. The hands of Hockin's clock had shown a few minutes of three o'clock. Dave had little more than a half-hour in which to cover seven-eight miles of broken country before hitting the stage-road at the point he had in mind.

And, as he put the game buckskin to the

narrow and sometimes dangerous trails, Dave grimly considered the possibility of Lack and Fiedler being on the scene. If they were, what would his own course be?

Could he uphold the law and hunt his own kid brother to the rope's end, or–

He plunged down the last gully, out on to the level ground which narrowed towards a fissure in the caprock. The buckskin was sweating and straining under the relentless pressure of Dave's hands and knees and as they burst into view of the stage road, horse and rider both gathered themselves for a final, supreme effort...

Now that the fugitives had lost sight of the stage-coach and the road itself, Frank forced himself to take the lead, desperately striving to wipe away, temporarily at least, memory of that last scene when Dave had gone down to the bitch-girl's gun, had lain there motionless.

All the blood seemed to have drained from Frank's body in those few awful moments, making it easier still for Emma to take the initiative.

But now things were different. He alone knew the escape route and the girl, so cool and callous awhile back, was now throwing him scared looks, occasionally glancing over her shoulder as Frank plunged his roan deeper and deeper into the tangled trails of the cañon country.

His mind was still partially numbed, what with the shock of seeing Dave shot, the killing of the stage-guard...

Perhaps it was this very numbness which shortly enabled him to cast aside his sick fears and bitter remorse. Their own lives now depended on his ability to reach Lobo Cañon without interference. Pursuit at the immediate moment was unlikely. It would take the stage-driver, whom Frank had recognized as Sid Machoff, some while to cut free the dead horses, fix reins and traces and get the coach rolling.

Even then, Machoff could do no more than head for town and report the hold-up. But, all along, the kid had not forgotten what Lack and Fiedler had said the other day – the day of Ma's birthday! And right from the time of starting out with Emma, he had kept ears and eyes open, half-fearing that at last luck would turn and confront them suddenly with the law in the shape of Herb and Will at the head of a posse.

He was thinking of all this as he rode, yet instincts were alert so that he did not once fail to react in time to an unexpected obstruction across the trail, or the sharply thorned branches of prickly pear.

As he slowed down to give the hard-breathing roan a blow, Emma spurred up alongside, reaching out to grab his arm.

He turned sharply, seeing the sweat of fear on her face, the near panic in staring eyes.

'Wait a minute, Frank!' she gasped, still holding on to his arm. 'We gotta figger out what we're gonna do! We–'

'We's headin' fer Lobo Cañon,' he told her roughly, 'like was arranged–'

'Sure! I know! But these hosses, Frank. Cain't we git rid of 'em, change 'em with some trader? They got descriptions by now–'

'We gotta take *some* chances,' he said coldly. 'An' we sure cain't turn 'em into blacks in a hurry, even if thet would help–' He broke off, eyeing her with bitter hatred as though, at last, seeing her for what she was.

'I'm thinkin' more about what you did to Dave – my brother – you gun-crazy bitch! Mebbe you even killed him–' His voice choked off in a racking kind of sob.

'I only creased him, I tell yuh! Yuh screamed out too late – even then I didn't know et was Dave. How could I? All I knew was some hombre was comin' to git us! It was him or us, Frank – you gotta see et thet way. Likely ef I had not shot, we both would be on our way to the pen–'

He broke free of her grip, tied the mouth of the sack securely, distributing the load more easily across the saddle-bow.

'You made your fust mistake, killin' Ed Stubbins, the shot-gun guard. You could o' winged him. Now we got a murder rap to beat. An' you'd 'a' killed the driver ef'n you was able to line your sights on him. An' I still don't know about Dave–!'

She built a quirly and lit it with fingers that shook. Anger was quickly replacing her former fears and she cursed with the fluency of a camp follower.

'Mebbe yuh'd 'a' sooner had yore precious Davy take yuh in an' let yuh swing! What kinda brother is he, anyway, actin' like he was a law-dog. Yuh allus tol' me yore folks was safe, not to worry–' She sneered. 'Well, Mister Hervey, mebbe yuh don't value yore pelt, but I shore do mine an' the sooner we git through Lobo Cañon an' back t'the arroyo–'

'We're goin',' Frank said softly, 'but there shore won't be any more jobs. You fixed that by killin' Ed Stubbins.

'We'll share out an' then separate fer good. We both gotta keep under cover till we kin quit the Basin. But if anythin' serious has happened to Dave–'

He kicked the roan into a gallop, the girl, after a momentary hesitation, following close in his tracks. The ground was easier here, enabling them to put on more speed.

They left the brush-choked twisting trail and burst out on to the base of a talus slope which lifted towards Lobo Cañon. Involuntarily, they both sawed on reins as they viewed the half-dozen or so riders strung out in an arc some quarter-mile ahead!

The clatter of shod hooves striking rock came clearly to the ears of Lack's small posse. Men swung round in the saddle and shouts went up as the dust-caked riders were spotted.

'*Wait, Emma!*' Frank choked. 'Mebbe we kin bluff them. That's the sheriff! He cain't know yet about—'

But Emma didn't hear him. She was sure enough in her own mind that the armed men yonder were out searching for the stage-coach robbers. How they had gotten the news so quickly or how they had been able to reach Lobo Cañon *ahead* of Frank and herself, she had neither the time nor the desire to figure out.

Sufficient that five armed men and a sheriff rode between her and freedom and, sufficient too, that ten .44.40 shells lay ready in the Winchester magazine at her right leg.

She had the roan steady as she whipped the carbine to her shoulder.

'*Hold et!*' Lack's voice bellowed out. 'We want—'

'*Fer Pete's sake!*' Dick Maury shouted. 'One of 'em's *Frank Hervey! Mebbe*—'

'They's fixin' to shoot, ain't they?' Lack snarled, whipping gun from holster.

Crack!

The Winchester barked and Herb Lack's

heavy figure jerked in the saddle, six-gun clattering to the ground as he clutched at his bloody arm.

The carbine swung round and barked again. A man pitched headlong from the saddle, his mount rearing up, bumping into a rider close by.

Again Emma's gun cracked and this time the heavy bullet screamed between Wildcat's gunsmith and Sam Platt the hostler.

These men were traders not gun-fighters, had been pressed into the law's service at the last moment. Maybe if Fiedler had been there, instead of out searching with another small posse, he would have given the men a quick lead. As it was, their surprise and shock coupled with a natural antipathy towards gun-violence, gave Emma the chance she had hoped for. Confident in her extraordinary gun-prowess, she had reckoned on dropping two or three riders, creating confusion in their ranks sufficient to guarantee her escape.

And, this time again, she had acted with astonishing and coldly-calculated swiftness, in no wise appalled at attempting more murders.

'Start shootin' yuh fool!' she hissed at Frank as she levered a fresh shell and triggered, knocking Charlie Schwarz's mount from under him.

Yet, even though the girl had fired four

shots, three of which had found marks, the whole encounter was no more than ten-fifteen seconds' old.

Frank's first instinct had been one of headlong flight. But, invisible strings had kept him tied to Emma's stirrup. He felt the see-saw tug of conflicting loyalties, urging him on the one hand to fight back, ex-horting him again to refrain from doing further damage and whispering in his ear to ride away and keep on and on and on...

He knew these men well enough. He and Dave and Ma had traded with them over the years. But in that moment of agonized doubt, a decision was made for him.

Perhaps the sight of Maury with a lifted rifle; perhaps that first glimpse of the hated Gil Blessiter's face, dark eyes peering along the sights of a carbine.

Frank scooped the Winchester from its boot almost before the echo of Emma's last shot had faded. But the desperadoes could not hope for further victories. The element of surprise, at first their staunch ally, was with them no longer and as the kid took aim, a veritable cannonade of fire burst from the guns ahead.

Even Schwarz, on his feet, had managed to retain his gun and loose off a bullet. Even the wounded sheriff, swaying in the saddle, was shouting at his men to burn down the outlaws.

Frank's shell missed the target he had aimed for but, ironically, it took Gil Blessiter in the neck even as Frank himself felt a seering pain in his left side. He knew he had been hit, though his body between hips and ribs felt numb after the first burning stab.

For all his waywardness, his get-rich-quick ideas, Frank Hervey was not a born killer. Not like the girl; she was a natural. Revulsion swept over him; not only because he had dropped Gil Blessiter, but at sight of the girl, sweat-streaked face white like the bleached bones of a long-dead steer, yet alive with cruel excitement, sharp teeth fully revealed against her thin, drawn-back lips.

But instead of firing again, she thrust the carbine back and lifted the reins.

'Now we got a chance ef'n yuh kin lead us *away* from the cañon!'

He nodded quickly, returning gun to saddle-boot and sending the mauled posse a last swift glance.

It looked like Maury wanted to follow, but the others were not of the same mind. *They've had their bellyful of killin'*, he thought, *and so have I!* He neck-reined his mount, digging boot-heels in with sudden savage determination.

Maybe there was still a chance to shake free, to share out this loot and then start up again in another territory; Arizona, even California.

Yet, after a half-hour of rough riding, he was rolling in the saddle, weak through loss of blood and the spreading flames of fire in his side.

It wasn't pity that prompted her to catch his reins and slow them up.

Only Frank knew these trails and, until they were safe from pursuit, *she had to keep him alive at all cost!*..

Right up until the last moment on Friday, Sheriff Lack had been stubborn about organizing a posse for something that was no more than a hunch; not even that maybe.

The most that could be said, was that there could be a slim chance the bank robbers might attack the stage somewhere between Belleville and Wildcat. That was always allowing they were still around the district and had not high tailed it days ago.

'Sure, I told folk mebbe we would sashay around the cañons,' Lack grunted, 'but only on account the sign led that way an' we gotta earn our *dinero* somehow. Wey's been shoutin' blue murder–'

'Don't yuh figger we stand a better chance, jest supposin' them bandits try fer the gold – with an armed posse at our backs?' Fiedler drawled.

'Yeah, sure! But we'd need an army of men was we to picket the hull stage road an' the cañons–'

'Let's git what men we can,' Fiedler countered, 'an' mebbe split ourselves up into two patrols. They's Gucht in town along with a few other Hatchet riders. We could—'

Reluctantly, Lack agreed…

From a high plateau they watched the winding ribbon of road, Lack and Fiedler with a dozen men grouped around them.

'Thar she goes!' Schwarz pointed to the match-box sized coach as it rolled along towards the last ten-mile stretch. Shortly it disappeared from sight round a bend in the road.

Sheriff Lack let out a grunt, half relief, half disgust.

'Ain't anythin' goin' to happen now, Will. Leastways not to the stage. Reckon we'll take a quick *pasear* over to Lobo Cañon – an' look fer any fresh tracks—'

'Sure seems like my hunch ain't gonna pay off,' Fiedler admitted, 'but if you got enough men 'case of any trouble, *I'm* honin' to ride around some—'

Lack could not resist a tolerant grin as he nodded, wheeled his horse and trotted away at the head of his small posse.

Fiedler stared after them for a minute, then turned and faced the impatient Hatchet riders, addressing himself primarily to Gucht.

'All I want, Munro, is fer us to make sure

the coach has reached town. We foller the tracks which same'll be fresh as a daisy–' He broke off suddenly, head bent to one side. 'Figgered I heard a shot, mebbe a couple–'

Gucht shook his big head and looked at Corrigan. 'Didn't hear anythin'. You, Butch?'

Corrigan grinned. 'Will's hearin' things. He'll be seein' 'em, next!'

'All right,' Fiedler said softly. 'Let's go!'

They faced quite a ride down from the plateau. Sharply descending, undulating country and, unlike the cañons themselves, stubbled with elderberry and chokeberry bushes and occasional clumps of juniper and piñon.

It made the going pretty tricky and even when two more shots rang out faintly this time, causing the Hatchet men to exchange swift glances with Fiedler, any great increase in speed was impossible.

Fiedler himself would not have chosen the plateau as a watching point for this very reason. *Likely,* he thought, *Herb hadn't relished the idea of havin' to climb back on his way to the cañons!*

It was a full half-hour before they were able to reach the road and start in following the coach tracks. Another twenty minutes before their tiring mounts carried them on to the stretch where the Belleville-Wildcat stage had been held up some three-quarters of an hour previously.

There was no sign of the coach itself, but what lay in the road provided instant and ample evidence that Will Fiedler's hunch had not been so far wrong!

A couple of dead horses, obviously a pair from the team, lay near to the middle of the road. Five-six yards away, was the strong-box, lock blasted and lid open to reveal its complete emptiness.

Over to the other side of the trail, Gucht spotted another dead horse.

'That's Dave Hervey's buckskin,' he said. 'What the hell's *his* horse doin' here and where's the bucko himself?'

'We'll find out all the answers presently,' Fiedler said quietly, 'when we reach town.

'Someone's taken the coach on with four horses, mebbe it was Sid an' Ed, mebbe Dave Hervey, I jest don't know yet.'

If I'd known Hervey was around here, Gucht thought viciously, *I might 'a' gotten the chance to square my account! Still, there's time yet to get the bustard an' pin it on those road agents!...*

CHAPTER 14

BLOOD OR WATER?

The lamps were alight in the Hervey house and Dave sat before a wood fire in the living-room, a clean bandage swathing his head-wound.

Ma's head was bent low over a pile of mending on the table – fingers moving mechanically, the lamplight playing on her pale and haggard face.

'You better tell me everythin', Dave. I gotta know sooner or later. I – I know a little, already!'

He nodded, dragging his gaze from the flickering logs and shaping a quirly.

He stuck the unlit cylinder in his mouth and, slowly at first, began telling her all he knew.

'Every small thing seemed t'add up, Ma, you see. But I still somehow couldn't figger Frank as–'

'I've wondered now for a day or two,' she said in a voice husky with grief. 'Ever since I knew about the Hatchet steer an' – an' Bart Kroeller!'

She nodded as Dave lifted his shocked

gaze to her face.

'I guess we both had our secrets, each tryin' to keep somethin' from the other. You knew, or figgered Frank was – was tied in with the bank robbery, an' I knew that he'd not only stolen a Hatchet steer, but worse'n thet – he killed a man! Yeah! Bart Kroeller, an' accordin' to Walt et wasn't even self-defence!'

'Then why–?'

'I guess this also has to come out now, but promise me you won't go off half-cocked, promise me–'

'Is it to do with Dillon?'

Again she nodded. 'Have I yore word, Dave?'

'If thet's the way you want it, Ma!'

She told him then of Walt Dillon's promise; her own promise which she had made gladly in order to keep Frank safe.

'You can't blame Walt,' she finished up. 'I guess he didn't do more'n a lot of men would do! He wanted to marry me – still does perhaps – an' that was the *only* way he could make sure of it!'

Dave stood up and flung his unlit cigarette into the fire. When he turned, Ma could see something in his face, in the bleak, implacable expression of his grey eyes, which she had never seen before.

Her heart seemed to stop beating as an awful fear, newborn now, clutched at her.

'You're not – not figgerin' on–?'

Dave said woodenly. 'He's an outlaw now, with a price tag of five hun'ed dollars; he ain't one of us any longer, Ma. He killed Bart Kroeller–'

'But Kroeller was a gunman, Dave! You know thet! You cain't call et–'

'It's murder, whichever way you figure it. If Kroeller had drawn, an' Frank beaten him, it would be jest a killin' in self-defence. There's a heap o' difference. Oh, sure, he could 'a' shot me too, out there on the stage-road, but he didn't. Jest let his murderin' mistress pull the trigger an'–'

'*Dave!* How can you say such things without you know fer sure? Sid Machoff–'

'Yeah! That's right enough. All Sid told me afterwards was one o' the bandits, the smaller one, was a girl. Mebbe I shouldn't 'a' said what I did–'

'*She* shot you *and* the buckskin; accordin' to what you said, but Dave, how – how did you know the other one was Frank? You said he was masked an' et wasn't your roan he was ridin'! Et was only later, when Herb got back with the story–'

'Herb confirmed it, yeah. The two of 'em had almost reached Lobo Cañon when they ran smack into the sheriff with five-six men. They musta figgered they was well away and natcherally, they wasn't wearin' masks.

'But even then Frank tried to kill again,

206

even if it was the girl who winged Herb an' dropped Fred Stokes. As to how did I know–' He paused, put a hand to his throbbing head. Some of the tight woodenness went out of his expression. 'I – I – well, Ma, I guess et wouldn't matter *how* Frank was dressed up or what hoss he was ridin'. Reckon I'd jest know him, thet's all!'

'Like a mother knows her own bairn!' Ma whispered the words under her breath, casting around in her mind for some way to save Frank still.

Dave looked at her, slowly shook his head. 'I know what you're thinkin', but et ain't any good. They's nothin' I wouldn't do to make you happy! Nothin' – except this!'

'But why've you gotta go lookin' fer him, Dave? Why cain't you let the law do thet? *Our job is to save him, not hang him.*'

He came over, placed his big arms gently around her shoulders, drawing her on to his chest and kissing the soft golden ringlets.

Presently she drew away. She had cried but now her eyes were dry.

'I doubt if Herb or Will *could* find him–'

'Then let him go! Give him a chance–'

'I ain't judgin' him, Ma,' Dave said earnestly. 'But men are bein' killed through Frank an' thet girl! D'you think it's fair to those men and their families – to leave him go free an' mebbe kill others?'

Ma sank slowly into her chair, her hands

clasped tightly on the table. Her eyes were closed and her lips moved as she silently prayed for help.

Dave watched her, wishing that *he* and not Frank were the killer. Then he moved across to a drawer, opened it and withdrew a belt and gun wrapped in oiled cloths.

He wiped the gun clean, methodically loaded the six chambers and buckled the belt around his hips.

'I'll haveta ride the mare into town an' get a hoss from Sam.'

Clovis Hervey did not reply. But as Dave slid the gun into its holster, she said quite matter-of-factly. 'They's a wagon comin', Dave, an' I think et's Frank!'

He stared at her in utter amazement before opening the door and stepping out into the night.

He heard the crunch of wheels and the clip-clop of hooves and, narrowing his eyes, made out the shape of a wagon and team across the creek.

He wondered who it could be driving up here at night and stood, half in the shadows, waiting until the wagon rolled into the yard.

'*Dave!*' Her low exclamation was no more than a whisper in the night as she drove on without pause round to the side of the house and straight into the shed alongside the Hervey's own wagon. Mystified, Dave followed and now, in the light cast from the kitchen window, he could see the pale, deadly tenseness of Sorrel Sperry's face.

'What's wrong, Sorrel?'

'Let's go inside,' she whispered, moving past him towards the rear door, faintly discernible in the starlight.

He only nodded, shepherding her through into the living-room.

Ma's fixed gaze was on the door and as they stepped into the brightly lit room it was she who had the first clear view of Sorrel, even before Dave.

There was blood spattered down the front of her dress, even on her neck and hands, and swiftly Ma rose and crossed the room to her. Dave whipped round from the door, his shocked glance questioning and anxious.

'Fer heaven's sake, Sorrel, what is it – are you hurt?'

Hurriedly she shook her head, lips trembling as she spoke.

'It – it's *Frank!*' she breathed. 'It's *his* blood! He's in the wagon wrapped up in blankets, sleepin'. I – I brought him over because – well, when I found him, he – he kept askin' fer you, Dave, an' Ma! You see–'

'I kinda felt Frank was comin' home,' Ma said softly. 'You're Sorrel Sperry. How is he? Fer God's sake tell me quick – why are we leavin' him–?'

Sorrel sank into a chair by the fire and

209

lifted her gaze to the Herveys. 'He – he's wounded pretty bad, Ma. I left him in the wagon because – well for one thing, I wasn't sure–'

'He's alive?' Ma's voice was deadly flat, the skin on her face seemingly stretched tighter than a drum-skin.

'Sure. An' we got the bullet out – me an' Aaron – but he's lost a deal o' blood–'

'I better go bring him in,' Dave looked across at Ma.

'Supposin' the sheriff–' Ma swallowed hard. 'They's lookin' fer him, Dave, ain't they? What if they come here an' start searchin'–?'

'Has Lack or Fiedler been out to see Aaron?' Dave asked.

She shook her head. 'No, I guess he hasn't got any reason to – not yet anyway. But another thing, Dave. I – I didn't quite know how you-all would feel–'

Ma whirled and snatched up a lantern, lit it and moved to the door. 'Reckon I'll need yore help, Dave.'

He hesitated, glancing at the girl before turning to join Clovis Hervey outside.

They were back within a few minutes, Ma carrying the lantern, Dave holding the limp, blanket-wrapped figure in his arms, laying it down carefully on the horse-hair sofa.

There was no hesitation now in Dave Hervey as he knelt beside the stirring figure

210

of his brother.

Quickly he pulled open the blankets and loosened Frank's shirt and belt with firm, gentle hands.

He swung his glance round to the red-haired girl as Ma leaned over and kissed the half-conscious boy's wet face.

'You an' Aaron done a right good job of bandagin', Sorrel. You say you got the slug out, but is the wound clean? If not–'

'It's clean, Dave. I had some nursin' experience in Albuquerque an' Aaron understands gun-shot wounds. We figgered that if we sent for the town medico–'

'Sure,' Dave murmured. 'Doc Curry'd have to report it to Herb, an' then–'

'We gotta save him, Dave!' Ma spoke the words through tightly clenched teeth. 'An' I ain't lettin' you nor anyone take–'

'Easy, Ma.' He straightened up, towering over the two women. 'They's nothin' much we kin do right now 'cept mebbe try gittin' some whisky down his throat, an' help him sleep.'

Clovis ran to the cupboard, withdrew a pint bottle and handed it to Dave. She beckoned the girl. 'Come an' wash up in my room, Sorrel...'

Twenty minutes later, cleaned up and refreshed with hot coffee, Sorrel Sperry gave them the story.

'Aaron had some stores and medicines to

freight over to a small rancher a few miles west of Caprock,' she explained. 'Then, as he was harnessin' the team, one o' them lashed out. The iron shoe cracked a coupla bones in his left hand so he couldn't rightly grip the reins.

'He figgered on postponin' the trip 'till the bones was healed but he was plumb mad not being able to haul out the stuff, 'specially the medicines—'

Ma got up and refilled the cups with freshly heated coffee.

'—Well, to cut it short,' Sorrel continued, 'I persuaded Aaron to let *me* take the wagon. He didn't like et but I kept on 'till he finally agreed an' drew a sketch-map showin' exactly the trails an' short-cuts I hadta take.

'I was mebbe five-six miles on the road when a hoss nickered right near. But there didn't seem to be anyone or anything in miles. I got a clear enough view all round but there jest *wasn't* a hoss thet I could see. I waited a while then drove on but – well, et kinda worried me so much I turned back. Guess et was as well, because after huntin' around some, I stumbled across a kind of dry wash, more an arroyo I guess.

'There was a hoss down there, a roan, Dave, with a J.H. brand an' Frank was lyin' a few yards away. I – I didn't realize it – it was yore brother – yore son, Mrs Hervey – an' I was too busy fer a while tryin' to git him in the wagon–'

'Was he unconscious at thet time, Sorrel?'

'Mostly, though he mumbled one or two things which afterwards began to make sense to me. He even walked a few steps, me supportin' him, but by the time we got back to the store, he was unconscious again.

'I had managed to tie the hoss's reins to the tail-gate an' after Aaron an' me had done what we could fer him, we got down to a little figgerin'!'

'You – you knew then who et was?' Ma whispered.

Sorrel shot Dave a swift glance and gently he nodded.

'I – I recognized him as the man I met on the sidewalk in town – the day the bank–' She paused, compassion for Clovis Hervey choking the words in her throat.

Dave said quietly: 'It was Frank all right. It had to be. Too many things added up. He bought the black dye off Aaron to turn a coupla roan geldings into blacks!

'Each time he rode out, either on a job or to meet the girl–'

'*Girl?*' Sorrel stared.

'We know Frank's pardner was some no good girl he found – Sid Machoff, the stage driver swore to it – an' I saw her too, along o' Frank– But mebbe you don't know, Sorrel, the stage was held up yesterday afternoon, the gold shipment stolen an' –

an' the shot-gun guard killed?'

Horror leaped into her widening green eyes. 'Not – not–?'

'Not Frank,' Dave affirmed quietly. 'It was his murderin' girl-pardner again. But you may as well know, Frank's hands ain't clean either. Aside from armed robbery he stole a Hatchet steer an' killed a Hatchet rider.' Dave drew a deep breath and looked across at the sleeping boy. 'They's both hangin' offences–'

'You – you really saw – him – on the walk, with–?' Ma's grief-stricken gaze fastened to the girl's face.

'It's true right enough,' Sorrel whispered. I – I'm sorry, Ma–'

'You brought him back home,' Clovis said, 'where he rightly belongs. You ain't got no cause to apologize!'

'I told Dave as much as I knew, Ma, about him carryin' a sack an' ridin' off with his saddle-pard. I described him near as I could remember, but I hadn't ever seen Frank, not as I knew an' it wasn't until I found him wounded in the arroyo, a J.H. horse along–' She avoided Ma's harrowing glance and looked across at Dave. 'Even then I – I couldn't believe – but I remembered all your questions, Dave, when we talked about the – the bank robber–'

'Did Aaron tell you to bring him here tonight?'

'We would have looked after him, nursed him,' Sorrel replied a puzzled light creeping into her lovely eyes. 'But like I told you, Dave, he kept cryin' out fer you an' Ma. We figgered it best to take the risk an' bring him home tonight–'

'Lack might have patrols out right now, mebbe watchin' this place, figgerin' Frank'll return–'

'I wasn't thinkin' only of *that* risk. I was thinkin' of his life! You see, Dave, mebbe you don't know this, but I gotta tell you an' Ma the truth. It's only right you should know that Frank's only got a fifty-fifty chance–'

'How can you be sure, Sorrel? Sure you've done a wonderful job, you an' Aaron, but a doctor–'

'I have done doctor's work back in Albuquerque,' Sorrel said again.

Clovis moved over to the couch and knelt down. She stroked the boy's head softly with her work-worn hands. She turned her gaze to Sorrel and then Dave, as though silently imploring for a miracle.

It was not until that moment that Dave Hervey saw exactly what he had to do.

He stood up now and lifted Ma gently to her feet.

'I'm ridin' into town an' see Lack, but not – not for the reason we was discussin' earlier on. I figger to throw him an' Fiedler clear off

215

Frank's tracks–'

A light shone in Ma's eyes as she looked up and a smile curved her lips.

'Can you do et, Dave? Can you make et stick so they won't come houndin' him – so they won't even know he's here–?'

'I promise you they won't take him, Ma,' Dave said in a barely audible whisper and turned and reached for his hat.

He saddled the mare, not caring that the roan Frank had ridden was now waiting at Sperry's.

A bright moon was lifting over a juniper stand to the east, silvering the scrub grass, touching the horns of some nearby J.H. cattle.

Dave reined in for a moment, letting his gaze travel slowly around the section. Those more distant stretches towards Crooked River and Hatchet were no more than indigo patches on a black backcloth, too far away to reveal detail even in bright moonlight.

But what he could not see with the eye, he pictured clearly enough in his mind, going over each ridge and wash as he recalled them through the intimate knowledge he had gained over the years.

After a while he lifted the reins allowing his mount to set its own pace along the trail to town, leaving him free to reflect on the things that might have been. Maybe one day, he and Frank and Ma could have had that big spread in some other county or even in that new territory of Arizona. Maybe Dillon *would* have paid seven bucks an acre for Spanish Creek, just so he could rope it in and clap a Hatchet iron on the scrubland. And, there was a girl called Sorrel, with eyes like soft melting emeralds and hair the colour of a satin chestnut. He cursed softly, trying to keep the bitterness from his voice as well as his thoughts. He couldn't even say good-bye to her, nor Ma either, *else they would have known he had no intention of returning.*

But where did all this get a man? Just no place at all. What was the use of complaining? The cards had been dealt and this was his way of playing them.

With Ma feeling as she did about Frank, there was nothing else he could do. Rightly or wrongly, that was how Dave Hervey saw the problem in simple terms; the basic principles of an eye for an eye! Frank had committed theft and murder. But Frank was a gun-shot case and if he were moved again, quickly, it was certain he would die. He might be prepared to pay for his crimes, if he were conscious, if he could walk and fork a horse. But he wouldn't want to be taken helpless like a rat in a cage. And Ma, she might go suddenly wild if Herb and Will rode up to haul the kid away. Ma was crazy about Frank. Whatever he did, for as long as he lived, she would go on blindly ignoring the right or wrong of the situation...

He began rehearsing his story for Lack. That would be easy enough once Herb had recovered from the initial shock. His semi-belligerent *bonhomie* would quickly change to contempt and anger. For the man who rode into Wildcat and gave himself up as the *instigator* of these crimes, the king-pin, the one who had *forced* his brother to rob and kill – that man would be loathed and despised, tried and condemned without hearing in the minds of every town citizen.

Maybe they would not weep over a Hatchet steer, nor waste sympathy on the gunsel, Kroeller, even supposing Dave 'confessed' to those crimes as well.

But, Fred Stokes, the likeable grocer was dead; Gil Blessiter was in a bad way; Lack's left arm had taken a slug intended for his fat body and first the bank, and now the stage, had been cleaned out! Normally law-abiding citizens had lynched men for far less than this catalogue of bloody crimes!...

The mare nickered suddenly, twitching her ears, and Dave instinctively reined in as two shadowy figures appeared ahead.

Even then he did not smell real danger, until Munro Gucht spoke. Tardily, he remembered he was still toting the six-gun with which he had resolved to hunt down Frank.

He saw then, in the moonlight, that Gucht's companion was Butch Corrigan and knew with a cold certainty this was no casual meeting on the trail.

The thing had been carefully premeditated and worked out by Gucht to the extent he had a 'witness' along.

Dave thought: *Somehow I gotta beat them. If they kill me now, Frank'll be right back where he was!*...

CHAPTER 15

THE MAN FROM SPANISH CREEK

Gucht said: 'So you're wearin' a gun for once in your life, Hervey. That's fine, it'll save us the job of plantin' one on your body!

'What you got to say, my gilded rooster? What's it feel like to know you'll be dead in a few minutes?'

'Should 'a' thought *you* could best answer that question, Munro.'

Gucht flushed, recovered himself to smile evilly.

'It sure ain't the Hervey's day is it, Dave? Now the whole Basin knows Frank was one of the dirty bustards – robbin', killin'! An' all the time, you an' Ma makin' out how *good* you are; honest hard-workin' settlers, huh?

'I warned you Frank was hot for Pearl, didn't I, Dave? How else could the kid hope to shine against Gil Blessiter!'

Gucht laughed. 'But I plumb near forgot, Gil ain't likely to be in any shape for love-makin', not for quite a while, Dave, on account of a slug through the neck–'

'Git to the point you white-livered skunk!'

Dave drawled the insult softly, schooling himself in the difficult task of maintaining an assumed coolness.

Calmly he reviewed his chances. If he could stay even as relaxed as this, maybe he had a chance – a very slim one! Yet, neither of these men were slow at the draw, and all along Butch Corrigan's right hand had rested on his thigh, a few inches from his gun. Gucht's hands, free of the reins, were ready to move, whilst Dave's fingers remained lightly touching the saddle-horn.

'Fer Pete's sake, Munro, why don't we let the so-an'-so have it an' git the hell outa here? He shore is askin'–'

'You can afford to let a condemned man shoot off his mouth, Butch,' Gucht replied with his loathsome smile, but there was a rough edge to his voice that hadn't been there before.

Mebbe he's gittin' riled, Dave thought, *but I ain't got much time left to think of somethin'!*

'Yeah, Munro, you allus was a white-livered skunk an' allus will be, I reckon! Like when you drew on me at Sperry's only *then* I wasn't wearin' a gun! As fer Frank–' Dave's laugh was so convincing that even in his anger, Gucht stayed his hand, dark, glittering gaze fastened on Hervey's shadowy face. '–Frank's safely outa the country where neither Hatchet killers nor Peace Officers is likely to find him! *I* should know, Munro, on account I put him on a fresh hoss an' told him where to head fer. Like I told him everythin' else he had to do – how to hit Blessiter where it hurt him most; how to fix the stage job–'

'*You*–?'

Surprise narrowed Gucht's thick-lidded eyes. For perhaps the space of a split second he was held by Dave's astounding story. And in that infinitesimal fraction of time Hervey staked everything on a swift and sudden suicidal act.

From the first moment, he had been playing for time, hoping that some unexpected interruption would occur; a chance rider show up, perhaps.

But the moonlit trail to Wildcat had remained quiet, no human sounds except the voices of these three men, the intermittent jingle of bridle chains as the horses

221

moved and the soft squeak of saddle leather.

Unnoticed by Dillon's men, Dave had withdrawn booted feet from the oxbows. Now, with his life hanging by a strand more slender than gossamer, he hurled himself sideways to the left, upper body momentarily disappearing from view behind the mare's head and neck, right leg sliding up over the shiny saddle.

His left arm struck the ground, partially breaking his fall as he clawed desperately for the Colt. A gun roared out, shattering the quiet of the night and a bullet tore into Dave's boot a breath-space before he was able to drag clear of the saddle.

He was almost full length on the ground, upper body raised and supported by his elbow. A second shot echoed out; the mare screamed, threw up her head and, with a convulsive reflex movement, collapsed in a juddering heap, threatening to pin Dave helplessly in the dust.

Just in time he rolled clear, the action bringing hand on to gun-butt. He drew, and thumbed back the hammer, narrowed his eyes as Gucht's next bullet tore through his hat, whipping it away yards behind.

Pain started up from the ankle where Corrigan's slug had ripped through his boot. He glimpsed the two mounted men, six-seven yards away and fired at Gucht's massive chest as the foreman drew back the hammer a third time.

The guns exploded almost simultaneously, but Dave had drawn his bead a second before the other. Gucht's big body jerked back, half-twisted, as the .45 slug slammed into his breast-bone.

Corrigan's horse was giving trouble and the man had only that moment thrown down again on Dave. But the muzzle-flash and roar of Hervey's gun and Munro's death scream sounding in his ear, combined to upset Butch Corrigan's aim. He might still have nailed Hervey's hide, except that Dave, a crouching shadowy shape behind the dead mare, had flung himself a yard to the left before arcing down with his gun and firing full at Corrigan's body.

Dave's head moved back suddenly, the Hatchet rider's slug scorching the bandana at his neck. Gun cocked and ready, he watched Corrigan, but neither Butch nor Munro would fight any more gun battles. Munro Gucht lay sprawled stiff in the dust, one leg caught up in the reins, and now Corrigan's body had slipped from leather. His horse shied away, nickering with fear, yet oddly, Gucht's mount stood firm.

Dave got to his feet slowly, like a tired old man. He stood looking at the handiwork which Fate had forced him to perform.

Brain and nerves and body seemed dulled and sapped of energy and, with painful deliberation, he returned gun to holster. Clumsily he built and fired a quirly.

His head throbbed more intensely now and when at last he moved, he became aware that boot and sock were warmly wet with blood. He steeled himself to tackle the immediate chore ahead, which was to climb aboard Gucht's horse and hunt for Corrigan's strayed mount.

It took nearly an hour of sweating work before both bodies were roped to the dead Corrigan's pony. His leg wound and the hard physical exertion gave him a light-headed feeling as he hauled himself into leather and pointed towards town, trailing the other horse with its gruesome burden, on a long rein.

It was nearing midnight when Hervey rode down Main and pulled up outside the sheriff's office. A light shining through the window indicated that likely either Lack or Fiedler was inside.

He climbed down stiffly, favouring his blood-soaked leg, and half staggered into the office, conscious of the surprised glances laid on him by the two law men.

So they're both here, he thought; *guess that'll save havin' to tell the same story twice over!*

Sheriff Lack sat with his left arm in a sling, coat sleeve hanging down.

'We was figgerin' to ride over tomorrow

mornin',' he grunted. 'Thought mebbe you might tell us somethin'—'

'He's bin hurt,' Fiedler said. 'Seddown, Dave, an' tell us who shot you in the laig. Better let me roust out Doc Curry?'

Dave's head moved gently from side to side. 'It'll keep. Right now they's more important things to do, an' talk about.

'They's a coupla Hatchet ponies outside, Herb, as'll need takin' back, an' Gucht an' Corrigan are tied across one of 'em.'

'Dead?'

Dave nodded, began to build a smoke. When it was lit, he said: 'They's worse to come an' you ain't gonna like any part of et!' He unstrapped the gun-belt placing it complete with holstered Colt on Lack's desk.

'Frank's outa the country,' he told them, 'an' won't cause any more trouble. I told him what to do and where to go, jest like I told him an' the girl exactly how to rob the bank an' hi-jack the stage gold-box!'

They stared at Dave incredulously and then Lack's sagging face flushed angrily.

'See hyar, Hervey! If this is yore idea of a joke—'

'Yore drunk, Dave!' Will Fiedler snapped. 'Git a hold on yourself—'

Dave's sober glance swung on to the deputy's face and something in those steady grey eyes caused Fiedler to catch his breath.

'I ain't drunk, an' what I'm sayin' is the

225

truth. We wasn't makin' enough *dinero* outa Spanish Creek, haven't been more'n scrapin' a living fer years. I figgered we wasn't gittin' any place. Y'see I had visions of runnin' a big spread, plenty o' good grass an' cattle, like – well, like Dillon f'r instance.' He paused, drew on his cigarette. He felt calmer now. Confident that he was beginning to put over his story, the way he had hoped.

'I ain't making any excuses, Herb, jest tellin' you that me an' Frank was sick of workin' from dawn to dark, seven days a week an' still nothin' to show fer it–'

'What about Ma?' Fiedler was still too shocked and stunned to accept Dave's story as yet, but a whole host of questions were piling up in his head.

Dave made an impatient, contemptuous gesture with his hand.

'Ma would sooner die than do somethin' wrong. You men know thet as well as anyone!

'This-all was somethin' entirely between me an' Frank an' the girl–'

'Who is she?' Lack pushed the question out through angrily pursed lips. Like his deputy, Herb was not yet sure whether this was some stupid joke or whether Hervey had gone crazy. Certainly, the man from Spanish Creek *looked* normal enough and was talking calmly – not screaming out his

226

story like a crazy man or a drink-sodden bum.

'Someone I found,' Dave lied glibly, 'who was already wanted by the law in two other territories.

'What I'm trying to tell you both is this. Frank didn't do any killin'. It was me an' the girl everytime–'

'He killed Frank Stokes, didn't he?' Lack demanded, angrily pounding the desk with his fist.

Dave gave a tight smile. 'How could you be sure from that distance, Sheriff? Frank's shots missed. The girl told me afterwards, braggin'–'

'So you met them after the stage-coach hold-up?' Fiedler said softly, catching up the gun and belt and dropping them beside his chair.

'Sure. I know them cañon trails. Without me they couldn't have got away. The girl's a born criminal with a mind of her own, but I *forced* Frank into this; threatening him with a bullet if he didn't play et the way I said. An' you got Sid Machoff's word it was the girl again, who killed Ed–'

'What's her name? You gonna tell us where we kin find–?'

'We never did ask her name. We called her Billy, thet's all–'

'How you know she was wanted if you never found out her handle?'

Dave shrugged wearily. 'She had some dodgers she'd pinched from some law office. They got a likeness of sorts an' reward details, but even on them there was only the nickname, Billy.'

'An' you say Gucht an' Corrigan is out there'– Fiedler jerked his thumb towards the street – 'dead, an' tied to the saddle. How do them two hombres come into this?'

'They don't,' Dave murmured. He looked at Fiedler. 'Gimme a drink, Will. I don't generally–'

Fiedler shot him a quick glance, hesitated, then produced a bottle and glasses from a cupboard.

'Reckon we could all use one,' he growled, pouring the liquor while the sheriff watched Hervey closely.

Dave downed his drink, shuddered and felt new life flow back into his tired mind and body.

'You c'n believe this or not, et don't much matter, but Gucht an' Corrigan jumped me on the way into town tonight.

'Et ain't got a thing to do with me plannin' these robberies, but again et don't matter a hoot. Anyway, I reckon Munro has had et in fer me since I hadta take him down in front of Sorrel Sperry.' Again he moved his wide shoulders in a disinterested shrug as the two law men lifted questioning gazes.

'He was annoyin' Miss Sperry when I

came in. Aaron wasn't there an' the girl was plumb scairt. I dragged Munro off an' we had a fight–'

'You licked him?' Lack asked.

Dave nodded. 'Guess he felt kinda small without his gun, an' Gucht never was the forgivin' kind.

'I should 'a' been on my guard, but – hell! I was thinkin' of other things. Ridin' in to give myself up, fer one!'

'Wal, Dave,' Fiedler drawled. 'We only got yore word but ef'n there wasn't any witnesses, guess we gotta accept et as self-defence, eh, Herb?'

The sheriff nodded. 'I guess he ain't likely to admit drawin' fust!'

Dave lifted his right leg painfully. 'Thet was the first shot fired as I slid outa leather. After that they both fired. They killed the mare an' I killed them, is all!'

'Why you givin' yoreself up?' Lack demanded. 'I don't mind tellin' you we didn't have a thing on you. You might 'a' gotten away with–'

'I didn't want you ridin' close-herd on Ma, pushing her with questions about me an' Frank. Besides which, Herb, I ain't a murderer by nature. I figured jest to steal, not kill, but – well–'

'That's what they all say when they's caught!' Lack growled. 'They didn't *mean* to kill – et jest *happened!*'

'I wasn't caught,' Dave reminded the sheriff quietly, 'but ef et's goin' to make you feel good, Herb, I guess I cain't stop you claimin' you brought me in–'

'What else?' Fiedler interrupted impatiently.

Dave hesitated. As far as Frank's safety was concerned, he knew he need not mention Kroeller's killing and the Hatchet steer. But, if Ma were to be free of Dillon's blackmail threat, free to lead her own life without being forced into marriage with a man she neither loved nor respected, then it was best for him to take the blame of that incident as well.

But, why should he throw his life away if there was a chance, however thin, of living?

Dave Hervey never backed down from a deal. Having made his decision, he was still prepared to go through with it, whatever the ultimate outcome.

Yet, without knowing the full details concerning Frank's shooting of Bart Kroeller, Dave considered that Dillon, or the law, might have a hard job *proving* murder, as against self-defence. There was still the question of the theft. Even *that* might be turned in some way, enabling Dave to plead 'a mistake', arguing that he had been chasing a strayed J.H. steer and had...

'I hadta kill Bart Kroeller,' Dave said slowly, 'but let me tell you, we still got enough brush-poppers on Spanish Creek without havin' to steal from Dillon. Several J.H. critturs'd strayed, one big mossy-horn in partic'lar, an' when I saw one like et, I jest nacherally figured it was a Hervey beast. Wasn't till I shot et, I saw the brand an' knew I hadta strip the hide.

'Kroeller came up an', well – you kin figger the rest! I ain't givin' myself up fer murder, Will, but fer robbin' the bank an' stage. They's been killin's, sure, an' I ain't aimin' to see any more innocent bystanders shot–'

'Bart Kroeller, eh? Wal, we don't know anythin' about him, 'ceptin' he's a tough gunny. Dillon ain't reported any steal or killin', but what of Ed Stubbins?' Lack said softly, 'and Fred Stokes?'

'Both went down to Billy's guns an' ef I knew where she was headed, you wouldn't haveta *ask* me! But I jest don't know. When I set Frank on his way, he an' the girl had long since split up!'

Lack chewed on that for a while and Fiedler said: 'Mebbe I had better get them Hatchet bodies down to Christie's parlour?'

Lack watched him go out and then turned to Dave, his eyes coldly angry.

'I reckon we gotta believe you, Hervey, on account nobody but a madman would walk in an' throw all this in our laps, if it wasn't true – an' you ain't that crazy!

'You willin' to write out everythin' as happened, jest like you told it, an' sign sech a document?'

Dave nodded.

'You realize that if you're charged with murder, the trial will haveta be held at the county seat? But, if it's robbery alone, we kin—'

Fiedler burst into the room, cutting short the sheriff's words. Will looked a mite shaken. He held a piece of paper in his hand. But what startled Lack and Dave Hervey even more than Fiedler's excitement, was the appearance of Sorrel Sperry right on the deputy's heels.

Will waved the paper frantically in Herb's startled face.

'Dave ain't guilty of nuthin'!' he shouted, completely disregarding the rule of two negatives equalling a positive. *'Frank was—'*

But Dave Hervey had quietly slipped from chair to floor in a dead faint...

The afternoon sun carried more heat than it had done for weeks as its westering rays slanted down on the town.

Will Fiedler stood sipping a beer in Cassen's Lucky Strike. The stage had just pulled out from the depot and the solitary traveller had headed straight for the saloon to refresh himself and peddle his wares if possible to Max Cassen.

232

'Sure is hot, mister!' he told Fiedler as he asked for his own brand of whisky.

Cassen shook his head, the cue for mister whisky drummer to open up his case of miniature samples.

Fiedler watched and listened with only casual interest, the man's sales talk going on and on until at last in desperation, Cassen put in an order.

The grinning traveller snapped the case shut and raised his glass to Fiedler, his glance moving out over the batwing tops as a rig clattered to a dust-raising halt opposite.

Will followed the other's gaze, saw Dave Hervey in checkered shirt, tight pants and long-spurred boots, a dark low-crowned stetson on his head.

On the seat beside him, sat a red-haired girl, radiant and lovely in a dress of green shot with gold.

'Some filly!' the whisky drummer exclaimed, smacking his lips. 'By Gregory! I'd shore like to—'

'Better not let the Man from Spanish Creek hear you talk, mister,' Will advised. 'He don't—'

'The hell! This is a free country ain't it, mister deputy? You sound like you're scared o' the guy! Why, he don't look so big to me. He ain't even wearin' a gun! An' what's this Man from Spanish Creek stuff?'

Fiedler set down his glass and hooked a lean finger in the drummer's coat, drawing him closer.

'Let me tell you the story,' he drawled. 'Mebbe then you kin figger a few things out fer yourself!'

He stared back at Fiedler for a moment, shot a swift glance to the striking-looking couple across the street and then nodded.

'Okay, shoot! I like stories if they're good!'

'This is good,' Will said softly, 'but I doubt the way you mean!'

He talked on and almost against his will, the itinerant pedlar found his attention held. He scarcely noticed that the rig across the way still stood there, empty now, waiting for the man and woman to return.

'So – so it was the guy's kid brother all the time, huh? An' – an' this Dave hombre figgered to take the rap on account he knew Ma was soft fer the boy an' – Hell! Don't that beat everythin'! Can y'imagine a guy turnin' himself in fer murders an' robberies he didn't commit – but say, how did they find out an' what happened to the kid?'

Fiedler smiled. 'Oh, sure, I didn't quite finish, I guess. Y'see, Miss Sperry, as is Mrs Hervey junior now, came ridin' into town, 'bout an hour or so after Dave gave himself up. She had stayed with Ma Hervey an' Frank, but soon after Dave lit out, Frank recovered consciousness sufficient to write a full confession. He had no way of knowin' Dave was takin' the rap, but he *did* know he was ridin' his last trail. I guess like so many of 'em, he wanted to try an' put things right. Anyways, Miss Sperry got to figgerin' out a few things, what with Frank dying an' confessin' and Dave riding off *having promised them he wouldn't let Frank be taken!*

'Cain't say whether she worked the hull thing out or whether she jest acted on a hunch. But whichever way you look, Sorrel's smart as a whip–'

'She rode out an' brought Frank's full confession to you an' the sheriff, right away?'

Fiedler nodded, his gaze back across the street. Dave and Sorrel had reappeared; were laughingly stacking goods into the back of the buckboard.

'Excuse me!' the drummer muttered, picking up his case and diving through the doors on to the street.

Fiedler moved across the room, watched as the man threaded through the late afternoon traffic and hauled up in front of the Herveys, a little breathless from his exertions.

'Mr Hervey! an' you, Mrs Hervey! Mebbe this-all is a little late fer congratulations, but a friend of yours, the deputy sheriff–'

'Oh, Will Fiedler?' Dave smiled. 'What's he have to say, an' what kin we do fer you?'

The man shook his head. 'You got it wrong, Mr Hervey! The question is, what can *I* do for *you*! First, I'd like to shake you both by the hand!' He grinned, as first Sorrel and then Dave took the proffered hand.

'It ain't often a drummer like me meets up with – with *yore* kind, Mr Hervey, an' I'm tellin' you it's bin a pleasure and–' He broke off, looking suddenly sheepish, his bombastic, stock-in-trade veneer suddenly gone. '–Mebbe I've learned somethin' today. I shore believe I have! Here, take this with the compliments of Stowe and Mellins!' He reached into his case and came up with a full-sized bottle of golden liquor, thrusting it into Dave's hand. With a quick, half-nervous nod, he retraced his steps back across the street as Dave and Sorrel climbed back on to the seat.

'One thing I didn't mention,' Fiedler drawled, emerging from the saloon and intercepting the drummer. 'Next time you book a stage seat through to here, don't fergit to ask fer "Spanish Creek", an' not Wildcat. We's fixin' t'have the town's name changed, on account of a hombre called Hervey.'

The man grinned. 'I sure won't fergit, mister, but now I think of it, there was somethin' else you didn't mention. What happened to the bandit girl; did you–?'

The deputy grinned and looked across at Dave lifting the reins.

'He took care of her,' Will smiled.

This Large Print Book for the partially sighted, who cannot read normal print, is published under the auspices of

THE ULVERSCROFT FOUNDATION